HOME RIVER

BY RODNEY NELSON

PUBLISHED BY
THE NORTH DAKOTA INSTITUTE FOR REGIONAL STUDIES
FARGO, NORTH DAKOTA 1984

Home River
Copyright © 1984
Library of Congress Catalog
Card Number: 83-63482
ISBN 0911042-28-8
Cover photo courtesy of the Nebraska State
Historical Society, Solomon D. Butcher Collection.
Only a portion of the photograph was used in the
reproduction.

B983-1996
Benjamin Cox, Cliff Table, Custer
County, Farm Scene, 1904.
Solomon D. Butcher Collection

CONTENTS

Chapter I.	Eastern Estate	1
Chapter II.	Paal's Case	11
Chapter III.	A Dumb Toy	23
Chapter IV.	Weather Change	28
Chapter V.	Two Lives	36
Chapter VI.	Common Sense	44
Chapter VII.	Vale's Edge	53
Chapter VIII.	Minuet in G	59
Chapter IX.	Soap and Iodine	65
Chapter X.	Home River	74

Dedicated to Ann

Chapter One was originally published in *South Dakota Review*.

I. Eastern Estate

Little Peter seemed so taken with the picture book, and his round eyes so begging, that she had to sit down and go through it with him. "What does this say now — *Gløtt af Norge!* My such beautiful scenes from Norway." They were at Papa's desk. His office, a rummage of books and papers, occupied only an end of the living room but dominated it. She inhaled the smell of ink with satisfaction. It reminded her of girlhood. A few of the stains on the oak top were as old as she.

"Is that Seattle?" Her son had turned to a picture of soldiers and flags and was studying it like an owl.

"No but it sure looks like Seattle, doesn't it? Let's see." Ida read the caption reluctantly: *"Karl Johansgate med Slottet, Oslo,* and over here it says, *etter velgjort arbeid for Norges sak, hjemmestyrkene på marsj mot slottet."* She was glad that Papa couldn't hear; her accent was terrible and her understanding worse. Thank God the captions had been translated into English. "That's a big city in *Norway*, and the name of the city is *Oslo*, far, far over the ocean. Those soldiers have been in the war and now they're marching to the king's house."

"Am I going there?"

Ida laughed and hugged his chunky middle. "Oh we're not going anywhere for a long time!" The little man had done so much traveling already, he just expected it to continue. He would have trouble getting used to its all being over; everybody would. Ida began humming the song that had followed her since the beginning of the trip, "When Johnny Comes Marching Home." This restored her — not that she had been worrying.

She even partook in her son's owl-like fascination. It was a large, well-made volume of black and white photographs that showed mountain after mountain and fjord after fjord in painstaking clarity. They saw tight wood houses that had roofs of living sod, a girl in peasant costume who stood in a fancy carved doorway, horses on a gray meadow that rose, farther, to a treeless ridge where patches of snow still clung, Asbjørn Ruud the ski-jumping champion winging over the crowd at Holmenkollen, and it all seemed lovely and reassuring; things were getting back to normal over there too. Peter interrupted her singing to demand to know what it said under some venerable town buildings. A woman sat reading there on a front stoop.

"Isn't that nice, though. 'As in days of yore' — *alt ved det gamle*. See, that lady is out by her house reading just like they used to in *olden times*." This photograph answered to something tranquil and deep in her, a kind of staunchness that the scene expressed more movingly than she ever could. Ida's mood had become so pleasant that she instinctively resisted yielding all the way to it. "Norway sure is a beautiful country, but our country is nothing to be ashamed of either," she added.

What was happening in the round, blond head in front of her? He had been mouthing words when he learned to walk, and that was early, and now he was taking a solemn interest in books — a typical Iverson, though he bore a different name. Peter would be four next month.

He stopped leafing at a picture he had looked at before. "Sacred trees," Ida was about to tell him.

Then the phone rang and the house waited to hear if it was one long and three short. It was.

Papa had been in the kitchen filling canisters to be sent to Norway. All during the German occupation he had been supplying relatives in Oslo with coffee and sugar, and it was Cousin Marie who had given him the picture book as a token of their thanks. The Germans may have been ousted — some, according to Marie's letters, at the end of a pitchfork — but even now it was hard to get by, and Papa's mailings continued. He stood up and lumbered to the kitchen wall where the crank telephone hung.

Ida shushed Peter and tried to be motionless with him. When O.H. Iverson stepped to the phone, no one had better stir. He heard poorly enough as it was.

"*Hellaw*, Iverson talkin'. . .Hah?!. . .Who?!. . .Oh. . .As vell as it can, I guess."

Little Peter was quiet; such an obedient child. She knew that Mama would be out somewhere, maybe sorting in the shed. If Papa had business in the kitchen, Mama never stayed for long.

"Hah?!. . .Oh you can come any time. . .Naw. . .That's awright . . .Awright."

He appeared in the doorway, a big man. He was not really tall, not with his hunch and his bullneck that stuck out rather than up from his shoulders, and not really wide, though sturdy-framed; yet there was something big about him. Posed there with only trousers and suspenders over his long-handled underwear, bald, mustachioed, unshaven and sixty-seven, he looked as huge as the round oak stove in the middle of the room. Perhaps it was how he moved or didn't move that created the effect of size.

"Villiam Verner is coming at two o'clock!" he said.

Ida didn't know any William Werner but she recognized Papa's tone as the one in which the sudden visit of a Langer or a Lemke or some other great politician had been announced when she and her sister and brothers were still children, and it meant all of them, including Mama, should keep out of sight. Papa had been doing his law business at home as long as she could remember, and this had always been a thing of dire precedence; he would *not* allow his bedraggled wife and kids to disturb a client or a guest. They were at most servants in the region he inhabited, and when they got out of line he treated them as such. At thirty-one Ida felt as she had at thirteen, cowed and a little guilty.

Nothing more needed to be said. His down-slanting blue eyes snapped with self-importance. He returned heavily to the kitchen.

"There's a man coming to see Grandpa," she whispered, "so he's got to get ready. Let's go outside for awhile."

Now there would be shaving with the straight razor, and if anyone dared to poke indoors during this ceremony, he would meet the wrath of O.H. Iverson.

They escaped by the front way, entering a lemon-yellow autumn forenoon that after the gloom of the house almost startled her. Peter wanted to take a walk but she said he should run and tell Gramma that Grandpa's going to shave; Mama would be angry to find the house closed at noontime; and he disappeared round the corner, knowing just where to look for his grandmother. The fall was late this year and not quite all of the leaves were on the ground. A perfect October, she thought, a real one — her first North Dakota autumn since 1942. She laughed at her reaction to Papa. You would think I hadn't grown up one bit! Still, it was nice to be like a daughter, to *be* a daughter, again.

The radio must have become a part of the ceremony, for she could hear it booming in the kitchen: *In a speech given at the dedication of a dam in Gilbertsville, Kentucky, today, President Truman said, "Let's all go home and go to work, cut out the foolishness and make this country what it ought to be..."* People had grown close to the radio these years, even O.H. Iverson.

Ida left the sloping porch and strolled a distance into the yard where stubble thrust at her ankles. They didn't mow here. The grass went wild from spring to whenever a neighbor took it for hay, and this season the cutting had been too early; the yard looked pretty rough. It wasn't so bad out on the drive. Papa's Model-A tires kept the grass down. But once there she could turn, arms folded, and survey the whole "estate." Oh, but the place was a mess!

This had been a farm like many another in the plate-flat Red River valley, a good-sized house with a barn and the rest of the necessary outbuildings set in trees which the original settlers had planted back in the 1870s. But an unmarrying lady had inherited ownership and chose not to live here, renting it out instead to a minister, and during the country parsonage time the barn, the chicken coop and several sheds had gone to ruin and soon were carted away. This left the house, one large "shop" behind it (which had become Mama's catchall) and one remote granary that was used by the man who farmed the land. Ida's parents had moved in around 1941. Rent was cheap: the depression was still on. As with every earlier place they'd had, Mama and Papa did little here to impede nature's work, and decay was rampart. Oh Mama kept up her flowers of course. Papa surely took his scythe to the ragweed in August. But they were getting older now too, and the law practice never did bring in much (if it weren't for the rent off the little acreage Mama's mother had left her!), and the war having removed their children, some to the army, some to marriage and Seattle, they had also been alone and she couldn't blame them.

The u-shaped grove opened east at the ditch of the township road. Far back in the central yard reposed the house. It had two stories and a dormer window over the porch, and though the porch had lost most of its railings, there were still lathed columns supporting its roof. The main building sat north and south, abutting a smaller part on the north; thus the house had three gables in all. Three gables and two chimneys and stained glass in the front door! Squinting, Ida could well imagine the elegance of which only the ghost remained — white walls, red trim, expensive curtains, a neat lawn. The unpainted, unkempt reality brought forth her wry streak, an Iverson characteristic to which the needy '30s had added an edge. It ran in all the kids. When her sister Bee had dubbed this place "the eastern estate," the name had stuck. Ida repeated the words and laughed sadly.

Well if you ignored the house with its gutters dangling from its eaves and the assortment of buckets and barrels that Mama had put below to catch the rain, then it didn't look too bad. The grove was nice. Three magnificent trees, an elm, an ash and a cottonwood, rose higher than any others where the yard ended to the north; the elm was already naked but the ash and the cottonwood bloomed gold against the sky. If you ignored the shabby Model-A parked underneath, you couldn't call the *rest* less than beautiful.

There was a derelict wooden tub at the foot of the elm and someone — Papa, she bet — had been leaving nuts in it. He shot rabbits but he loved squirrels. Then one of Mama's shallower rain-pans, by the house, was half full of leaves and the water, through days of sun, had taken on a brownish hue. It smelled like a kind of tea. Ida paused at these two exhibits on her way to the shed. She couldn't say just why, but the simple fact of them was comforting.

Mama was preparing her cardboard boxes for winter. She had set them in a ring on the grease-soaked earthen floor so it would be easy to tell what had gone into each one. She talked as she worked, perhaps to herself, perhaps to her little grandson who sat yawning on a ruined sawhorse.

"When am I ever going to have room for all these things? Here's the pen that Alvin was to have, can't throw that out, never know when he might need it. I'll put it in with the candles Martha made. What's this? *Nei* this should have been with the other pictures. Better bring it in the house so it don't get wet."

Some chips of dull violet indicated that the outsides of the shed had once known red paint; now they were colorless. Of the interior hardly anything could be seen. The panes of the one window had been knocked out long ago. The door hung open for light. As Ida stepped inside she reminded herself to tell Peter to watch out for nails.

Mama and her boxes formed an island of activity. She looked more preoccupied than usual and when she wasn't talking, her lips came together in a hard line. "All this stuff and no place to use it. Here's the old album that should have been in the front room, but they don't want things in the front room unless it's their own junk, and so it has to sit out here in the wet and the mice and God knows what. Have you ever seen the beat!"

Shaving may have been Papa's ritual but Mama had her own and that was sorting. She loved to put on an ancient felt hat which had lost its band and come out and sift through her treasures by the hour, for these boxes contained all that her relatives, living and dead, had given up and that she would keep until the dusk of her days, and while sorting she could try to think of someone who'd need a perfectly good blouse or wallet before then. If Papa had been able to provide her a house, if he'd even been more generous with the space in the ones they'd had, then maybe she could have gotten along without her boxes. There was a hint of protest in her activity. But mother and daughter were close and Ida knew that if Mama seemed upset, it had only a little to do with the last sorting of the year; it had quite a bit to do with the immediate plans of O.H. Iverson.

"Peter, have you been helping Gramma like a big boy?"

"I'm *in* here," he explained.

"And how's everything coming?"

He put his hands on his hips and scowled. "It looks terrible!"

"Nay would you listen to the kid!" said Mama. "He's just like me!" Both she and Ida laughed.

Peter had not been trying to be funny, and the women's laughter was unsentimental. Theirs was poverty humor, hard, fatalistic, and always at its best when turned in mockery on themselves, expressive too of a belief that what people get they somehow deserve. Jensine Iverson had inherited more than a small tough body from the Scandinavian peasants; she had received the widsom of those who for centuries had been learning to do without. When she was a girl on the North Dakota frontier, life had not seemed easy; yet according to her parents things had been much worse in the old country, and one should therefore be thankful of the gift of life itself, showing one's thanks in work. This she had done. But in 1913 she had erred in marrying a *fritenker* man who only scorned the ancestral wisdom; and while her sisters and friends were achieving something, she had been held in poverty with five kids to raise. (Divorce was unthinkable; the most she could do was to kick lawyer Iverson out of her bed.) Thus Jensine was readier than some for drought and depression. The American '30s had merely lent bitterness to her character — not that she'd ever thought of this world as anything but a vale of tears, just that there were so many like her husband who chose to complain and prophesy instead of working. Bitterly, she had atoned for such iniquity by the sweat of her own brow; this showed in her gnarled limbs, in the rags she wore. But she also had sweetness in her. What she denied to O.H. Iverson she gave fully to others, to her children in particular and now to her first, dear grandchild.

Ida had no doubts of their welcome here. She and Peter and even Paal could stay until doomsday if it came to that, God forbid. However, there were still the concerns of the moment to attend to. Mama's laughing had loosened her upper plate. This fixed, she had set her mouth in a straight line again.

"I suppose Peter and I could be upstairs or outside while that man is here." Ida spoke too softly and had to repeat it.

"Oh they have the whole front room and certainly that'll be enough!"

"They" meant Papa, the undeserving. Whenever he interfered with the needs of the deserving, Mama would turn pitiless. She sat in the grubby half-light and shook her head at the boxes. "Not only do they shut you out of the house at dinnertime, they don't want you to do anything in the kitchen all afternoon, just think of it! When do I get done with *this?* And Peter is getting hungry too."

"I can fix something for us later, don't worry," Ida said.

She lowered her eyes in deference to Mama's anger, but also to what she couldn't help feeling for Papa. Others were more successful all right and maybe he did act less than kindly to those around him, but he sure was intelligent and he said what he thought. Deep in Ida was a hurting shred of love for her father. While she knew that Mama's rage was justified, it was like an assault on part of her as well; it made her confused. Defending him would be the same as defending her inadequate self, so she tried to ignore the whole thing.

Mama thought, Peter rode the sawhorse, Ida waited.

"Will he be here tonight then?" Mama sounded rather distant.

And "he" meant Paal, who in Mama's estimation didn't stand much higher than O.H. Iverson. When Ida married him in 1941 there had been weeks of silence followed by weeks of angry lamentation: oh that one of Jensine's daughters should have made such a fatal mistake, oh that she should have committed herself to such earthly suffering! Mama no doubt had reason to oppose the institution of marriage. Would *any* man have been acceptable? Ida often wondered. Her baby's arrival in the fall had brought about a truce and there had been a Christmas reunion at the eastern estate. But if she and Paal had been the only ones to leave for Seattle, or had they chosen to stay there after the war, *then* they would have been outlaws. Mama wanted her kids in North Dakota.

Perhaps it was because Paal had returned her daughter and grandson to the land where they belonged that Mama no longer seemed quite so disapproving of him. Her mouth had even gone sweet again. Ida realized that her hidden affections were not now under attack.

"Ya he should be around," she said. "He had to see about a job this afternoon but I expect him for supper."

The day was going to be warm, too nice to waste in the bleak shed. This must have occurred to Mama also, for dusting her hands she got up from the overturned milk pail she had been sitting on and said it was time to go in and see if "they" were ready. Peter jumped down. As the three of them moved to the door, both Ida and Mama told him to watch out for nails.

Two o'clock must have come and gone unawares. Alone at the dormer window, Ida suddenly knew that she had been listening to men's voices for some time. She hadn't seen William Werner drive up or get out of the car. But a well-kept sedan sat in the yard as plain proof.

"Ya vell if Lemke has anything to say about it, the OPA is done for."

"You may be right, Mr. Iverson."

So she had fallen asleep anyhow. She remembered climbing the stairs with Peter to find one of his toys in the bedroom, then he had run back down to Mama and she had wanted to rest her eyes for a minute. Apparently she had walked in her sleep to check if Papa's visitor was here yet. That's what moving fatigue does to you!

Now it was like waking in a different place at a strange time. She might have been having a nap in Seattle and just dreaming the voices; it was like thinking about home instead of being home. The day too, which had broken sunny, was showing changes. She looked out the window at the sky over the river woods, which hedged the horizon a quarter mile east, and it was all bright gray. The view seemed to be an almost unfamiliar picture of itself in black and white, yet she knew this corner of the earth if she knew any. Oh yes, it reminded her of the photos in that Norway book, that's where the skies were so milky.

Something clanked downstairs. Papa was knocking his pipe on the ashtray.

"I might throw my own hat in the ring in a couple years."

"You *knaw*, the NPL isn't vhat it used to be."

Ida didn't try to pick a meaning out of the sound of the words, she just accepted it as background. Men's voices, whether in rooms or on radios, were distant from the little she knew. During the war they had interrupted her favorite soap operas with the tumult of battles and beachheads, and while she hadn't resented this — Uncle Sam didn't have a more loyal niece — they had awed her. They expressed the terrible importance of the far world. What they spoke of concerned everybody alive but in fact showed the helplessness of each meager person in the midst of it, so when really big news came she had been almost apathetic. Did it matter if she laughed or cried? *The force from which the sun draws its power has been loosed against those who brought war to the Far East.* And that had been the President!

The eastern sky brought thoughts of Seattle and how many afternoons she had looked at it there. Ida particularly recalled September, only weeks ago, and the great excitement beginning. The rest of them caught it from Bee and Lester, who were the first to decide.

The war's end celebration was done. There were no more dirigibles over the city and few welcoming parades, instead now there was a calm on everything, a smile in the air itself. They had all worked hard, gone without butter and meat and decent shoes, and that had been fine as long as the job had lasted; in September they saw it was finished. One afternoon Bee called to say they were packing up. Soon Oliver knew about it, and Lyle. Was it then or on another day that she began watching the eastern sky? Those afternoons were so full of the joy of getting ready, she didn't have many a pause for reflection; yet the sky was always there, saffron clouds towering in the dark blue as their signal home.

It was as though she hadn't appreciated the beauty of Seattle until it came time to get rid of the worst furniture, buy a car and leave. The light seemed to spread over the bay and the urban hills and the mountain ranges like an enchantment. She felt Seattle was putting on a display that said, Behold what you're surrendering.

North Dakota had been death-quiet in '43, a place for old folks. They had come west as out of darkness into day, first Aunt Martha and Uncle Aaron, then Oliver, Edith and little Ted, then Bee and Lester, herself and Paal and the baby, and finally her youngest brother Lyle when he got his discharge. Mama had spent both winters with them; even Papa had made a lengthy visit. Oh but hadn't it all been fun — the ferry rides to Bremerton, the trips to Mount Rainier! The men had found good jobs too. V-J Day was unexpected. Soon after, there was a warning in the newspaper, *5,000,000 may lose arms jobs*, and Paal was threatened with layoff at the shipyards. North Dakota beckoned. Mama's letters told of one happy reunion after another and the land reawakening. Thus the big decision. If she were to stay she'd have only Martha and Aaron, who were too settled in to move anymore; her dearest and best would be answering the call.

She remembered her parting tears, shed not so much for Aunt Martha as for the salt air of Seattle. As they headed east over Lake Washington, Peter was murmuring the theme song of the hour, "When Johnny Comes Marching Home," and she thought of the promised return of her second brother Jim, the only one of the boys who'd had to serve overseas, and of how many Johnnys were on the road this month. Her son's cheerfulness helped her, Paal's too. Paal sure seemed elated. She had never seen him grinning like this. He joined in the singing and it wasn't long before she chimed in as well. Yet those tears were hardly dry.

They drifted through Washington and Idaho, ushered along by the sun, and wherever they looked was paradise. Every green mountain slope offered welcome; in the Rockies the next was always lovelier. They ascended Lookout Pass in early evening and she and Peter saw a ranch grow smaller in the valley below, shadow filling in from the quiet mountains, the white of the barn going out, shadow surrounding them as they rose, and then it was Montana, another state, and another beauty left behind. Nothing to be sad about, but she cried anyway. She also cried a few evenings later as they rolled from the plains into the Red River valley. It was near dark and home lay huge and flat and purple before them.

"See, Peter? Now we're gonna drive into the *ocean!*" Paal teased. He was grinning as usual and meant no harm, but his son must have had terrible memories of the Pacific. There were more tears than Ida's to wipe, and in the laughing and the comforting her melancholy disappeared.

From Tower City on they had a short night journey to the yard of the eastern estate, to Mama's form in the open doorway, lamplight in the window, shouts and embraces; and the same old iron wind of North Dakota urged them indoors to Papa's tobacco stench and the friendly disarray of the kitchen.

Time since then had clipped by. Everything was as Mama said it would be. The young people were returning, servicemen and civilians alike, each with a lot to tell and do. Some hadn't come back. Those who had, wanted only to make themselves a life here in the place which the constraints of war had taught them to appreciate. They had seen the press of death in the cities of Europe, and in American cities, the press of living. Now they stretched their lungs in the Dakota wheatland, where there was room for all and hope enough to go around.

But while the gaiety continued the hotels filled up and rentals vanished from the market. The newspapers declared a housing shortage. Bee and Lester, first to arrive, had been able to snatch what Bee described as the last available closet in Fargo. It seemed Ida and Paal would really be up against it. He had already had to go looking though he was still worn out from the move — all three of them were, God knows — and then Oliver and Edith and Ted were supposed to be getting in next week. At least there'd be space at Mama's for awhile.

"Vaht they should do is break vith the Republican party!"

"But this here is North Dakota, Mr. Iverson, we can't forget that."

No beckoning saffron clouds today, she thought. The thin sky over the river told her she was home. By tomorrow Seattle would be like a picture in an album and she'd stare at it as though she had never walked those beautiful heights. A picture of Norway would seem no less unreal.

Ida had few regrets, she was just so tired. It would have been nice to take it easy and forget about houses and jobs and the rest, letting things come in their own good time (and indeed it *was* nice to have somebody else looking after the housework for a change), but she simply didn't dare relax.

Paal was kind and easygoing but he sure needed encouragement sometimes. Getting him to Seattle had been hard, he liked the prairie so much, and getting him out to work there had been a heroic accomplishment. Oh he had done all right, you had to admit, what with his injuries and illnesses and dark spells; they had managed to survive. He would even have stayed on at the shipyards, she bet, if there hadn't come that layoff notice. But there had, and he was cheerful again. "Well I'm through," he had said, merrily taking a beer from his lunchkit, "and I *think* I qualify for unemployment compensation!"

Poor Paal, he lacked the ambitiousness of other men, her brothers for example. She hoped he would be a little happier in North Dakota. Yet she feared the going would be rough. Not only was there a housing shortage, there were many people looking for work. What chance did *Paal* have? Uff-da, it would be nice to shut out the world and read to Peter and help Mama with the dishes, to have time on your side; she could certainly use a couple more weeks off; but time was against her, soon it would be snowing, and if she let up on him now they might never find a place.

The gray cleared and autumn colors reemerged as by the flick of a switch. While she didn't experience a similar transformation of mood, she did feel her old strength returning. The voice of the peasant ages told her to quit worrying and be thankful that she had a life to live, not to mention a husband and a fine young son. Be glad you were spared *real* hardship, it added.

Ya they would come through and that's all there was to it! She wanted to laugh but Papa and his visitor would have heard; so she smiled long and doggedly out the window. Things could be worse, girl. Here she was in a magnificent October; as the song said, it might as well be spring.

II. Paal's Case

The river is not a river, though its major source, the Otter Tail, coming out of the damp hills of west central Minnesota, deserves the name. The Bois de Sioux, its inconsiderable other source, trickles north from the Lake Traverse divide, but whoever called it "Sioux Woods" must have been joking or a third-rate poet: along those banks a tree is as rare as an Indian.

The valley is not a valley but one immense floodplain, the bed of ancient Lake Agassiz, and the Red is in fact a drainage ditch. Where it begins in the joining of the Otter Tail and the Bois de Sioux at Wahpeton, the trees begin also, and from there on the Red looks very much like a river. The steamboats used it as such, prowless, truncated vessels that had been designed for its uncertainties of width and depth. That was in the 1850s and '60s, when trade followed the waters and before Jim Hill came through on his iron horse. To get into Dakota Territory he had to bridge the Red. The steamboats, Jim Hill and the Territory are gone now but the ditch remains, providing a serrated eastern border for the state of North Dakota, widening into Canada to its expected terminus at Lake Winnipeg, then emerging hundreds of miles north as the Nelson which ends only in Hudson Bay. It's one of the few American rivers to flow in that direction; but in spring when all the meltwater and fallen rain make it into a huge mud puddle, it seems to be going nowhere.

The big settlement occurred in the 1870s, '80s, and '90s and most of the settlers came from northern Europe. They weren't exactly lured here; Dakota just happened to be the boom-land of the time. Those who homesteaded on the floodplain suffered in the absence of hills and trees through the harsh windy winters, but they soon discovered that the black soil under them was some of the richest anywhere and they might do well to stay. Thus they abode in the Red River valley, Germans and Yankees and whatnot at the south end, Poles and Canadians and Icelanders at the north, and in between, over the long stretch from Abercrombie to Grand Forks, a ruck of Norwegians. Thus many prospered.

Not all did, however. O.H. Iverson lost his father's farm. He gave up a good beginning law practice in Williston to come home and help the old man, but a married sister had already done him out of the place. After that it seemed he just went on giving up, and he was forty and learned. In certain cases the pioneers had too little land and too many kids to divide it among, so the farm would go to the best domestic politician in the litter, and in others it was the depression that took people away. Iverson was landless but he stuck around, moving with Jensine and the children to a different ramshackle house every three or four years and dawdling in law and politics until he arrived at the eastern estate at the start of his old age.

The Red is not red. It may have run that color awhile in 1862 as the uprisen Indians besieged Fort Abercrombie, but soon it would have resumed its usual umber a few miles downstream, close to where the Iversons now live. Better to say north than downstream. In country this unhilly, a stranger would have to check the current in order to tell down from up.

Twenty more miles north along the Red is Fargo, a large town now in 1945 and about to get larger. When Paal Malmlund said goodbye to Ida this morning they both understood that he would be driving "up" to Fargo.

His old Pontiac coupe had been seen in various parts of town. It was an eye-catcher with sidewalls and a rumble seat; moreover, he had Washington plates. They didn't know him here but they would turn and look anyway, thinking, Well there goes a man who's been out in the world and done a few things. The Pontiac had a rattling body and the paint job could have been nicer (he had painted it himself with a brush, later touching up the sidewalls too; what the hell, it made no difference unless you got right next to it), but it was a good car.

Ida's sister Bee had found an ad in the papers — room to rent, gas hotplate, share bath — and had given him the address on the back of an envelope. Bee and Lester were all set up in town and could help search, and he only had to follow the leads. So he parked his almost shiny black coupe on a street in north Fargo and approached the house number that matched the one on the envelope.

An expressionless woman in a duster answered his knock. At first she didn't say a thing and he wondered if she was ill.

Paal was a lanky six-footer and his long dark hair had a natural wave to it. He didn't have to try to be charming; his appearance and his slow, friendly manner took care of that for him. All he had to do was present a twinkle and a half smile and she'd like him soon enough.

"Ya they say you got a room available, I hear."

The lady of the house nodded and managed to invite him in. It was a fancy place but the shades were drawn and he could smell illness or worry everywhere; the room in question reeked of it. He listened to her monotonous description without interrupting. There would be no other tenants, just the owner herself, and he'd be using the front door, and bathroom articles would be supplied. No drinking or loud noise, that she couldn't tolerate.

She's got a cute mouth, he thought. Too bad she's not feeling better.

When she finished, Paal said he sure wouldn't mind living here, it was just the place, and strange nobody else had gotten to it before him.

The woman had been relaxing a little but now it seemed she was going to cry. "Oh I didn't know till this week," she said. "I was waiting for my husband to get home, in case he wanted to sell. He was overseas, you know, missing in action. Well I finally received the notice so at least I know he won't be coming, and I'll need the rent. If you want it ——"

She recovered, though; Paal was spared embarrassment. His click of the tongue might have indicated either deliberation or sympathy. Rubbing his ear, he looked at the figure in the linoleum.

"Ya I see," he said.

He knew that the room was his — not to mention a grieving widow. It'd be tricky to avoid committing himself without seeming to refuse. He could simply walk out on the deal and say he had been too late; Ida would believe him. But then he would have to dig around for another place to show her.

"You can't find a room like this every day, that's for sure," he said. "I'd really hate to pass it up. But I tell you, I have to see a man in Moorhead who's got an apartment. I promised I'd be there. Oh I spose I could skip it, but I don't like to make people wait. So if you think you can hold it a day."

"That would be possible, I guess."

She watched him with guarded interest. He smiled full strength, congratulating himself on his knack for getting along with others. This one was easier than he had thought. She had a cute nose too.

"I'll come back in the morning then. Bout eleven all right?"

Fine, there was no big rush, she'd see him tomorrow. It was almost hot inside the car in the summery forenoon. He put a wad of snoose in his lower lip and turned the key. Well that girl's in for a surprise! If she wanted to know about his marital status she could have asked, couldn't she? It wouldn't be *his* fault.

The engine idled unevenly. He was glad he had the tool chest locked in the rumble seat and that he knew how to take care of machines as well as people. Either might give out any time.

Paal had not been looking forward to this search; he'd had his fill of mad rushing in Seattle. At least now he could tell Ida that he had set up an appointment, and that'd keep her happy till eleven in the morning. They'd never rent the room, of course. So what? He would handle that situation tomorrow. Today he had just one more thing to attend to, applying for a damn job, and when that was over and done with he could knock off.

After a leisurely tour of the west side, the coupe pulled up at Magnuson Freight Company. Paal had dropped his wad in the gravel and headed for the office. They seemed to have quite an operation here, even their own shop. The high doors were open and he could see two mechanics working. It was twelve twenty. If the men had to stay through their noon hour, this must be a tough outfit. He'd better turn tail. But chances were the boss would be out to lunch so he had nothing to lose; and they couldn't say he hadn't been here during working hours.

However, Carl Magnuson was not only in but pleased to see him. Paal sat down in the offered chair knowing that this brisk middle-aged boy would be a hard one to manage.

"Yessir, we need someone for town deliveries. I hope you can drive?"

Paal said that he could; he could also repair engines and he had a wife and child. It wouldn't hurt to build up a case for himself, he thought.

"Family man! Wonderful! So the army didn't getcha, hah?"

Sensing a threat to his independence, Paal had been feeling morose — though he was careful not to let it show. His face had been the picture of geniality. Now, at the very instant of hiring, he was offered salvation. He was in charge again.

"Well I did go to enlist," he said, drawing the words out, "because I thought I should do my part like everybody else. But this here army doctor said I had a weak back, so I got a 4-F and that was it."

The owner of Magnuson Freight Company looked confused. "That right, a weak back? I don't know. There's quite a bit of lifting."

The applicant seemed undiscouraged. "Oh I can hold my own with the best of them. Long as I don't lift the wrong way I'm fine."

"Here I was about to give you the job, but I don't know."

Outside it was mild and fresh. The dusty office windows hindered the light. Unless Magnuson ended the interview in two minutes, Paal would have to do it for him.

But from there on it went easy.

"I guess I'd rather not take a chance on it. I don't have anything for you in the shop either. So why don't you give me your name again and where I can reach you, case I have an opening."

Magnuson had the usual trouble spelling the name. Other odd troubles showed in his eyes. Paal, already standing, was able to leave on a pleasant note:

"That's with a double *a*, how the old timers wrote it. I spose I could have changed the spelling but I figure if I can live thirty-six years with the name I've got I can survive a little longer. *Tusen takk* then!"

Starving for air and a pinch of snoose, he hurried to the coupe. This time he didn't let the engine warm; no sense hanging around where he didn't have any business. He had checked off both items on his mental assignment sheet, the room and the job, and as far as he was concerned the quitting whistle had blown.

One success out of two tries wasn't bad. He had given the fellow every opportunity to sign him on and the man said no. Well Carl Magnuson and all these bigshot trucking operators would just have to get along without him. Ida might be disappointed. But as he viewed the ugly freight docks and garages of westside Fargo his thought was piss on it.

He arrived downtown with a whole free afternoon ahead of him and parked at the Amidon Bar. The sunshiny streets were crowded. He wasn't much of a drinker but right now the ooze of snoose was only half a satisfaction; he should have a beer to complete it.

Paal Malmlund had been born in the Sheyenne River valley, way west of the Red and its floodplain, a sightly if unassuming landscape with hills and marshes and even some groves. He was raised on the farm, the oldest kid in a batch so large that he'd often forget the number, and he had always understood the meaning of work. A country boy had to be a mechanic and a veterinarian as well as an agricultural engineer. But everybody knew each other and they were all in the same fix, so there were neighborly fun-times too, barn dances, shivarees, *julebakken*, and at home was an assured family closeness. A trip to Valley City seemed like going abroad. Once his dad took him along to an air-show featuring the eminent Non-Partisan Leaguer A.C. Townley, and he was wonder-struck at the machines and the speeches both. He had rarely heard English spoken before. He and his parents and brothers and sisters talked in Norwegian. Who didn't? Oh his teacher had learned English at normal school and wanted to get the kids to try it, but she was from Lillehammer herself.

His father died young in the epidemic of 1919 when Paal was just ten. Life had always been toilsome but it had hung together at least; now it came under a shadow. Dad had forgotten to tell him the why of being born and living. His confusion turned to resentment when his mother up and married that ornery hired man. Well she did attempt to explain it to her eldest beforehand, how a woman with kids could not get by alone on the farm so it can't be helped and he shouldn't blame her, but since his dad and he had never had any use for that ill-tempered fellow, her words only seemed threatening. The shadow increased. From that day on he had little to say to the woman who had borne him.

The new step-dad didn't think much of Paal either and he had to endure shoutings and beatings until he got clever at handling the sonofabitch and then grown enough to stick a man-sized fist under his nose. He was a man in all but years when he left school at the end of the eighth grade. Reading books and sitting next to pretty classmates seemed like a worthier occupation than slaving on a farm. But his duty was with the cattle and out in the fields and that was that. Oh they couldn't stop his learning altogether; he needed some explanation of what happened, so he'd be up by candlelight till the pages got blurry. Meanwhile, babies kept appearing in the bed his mother shared with the ex-hired man, and Paal dreamed of going away.

He stayed, however. Two of his brothers were coming into their own as men and snoose-addicts, and maybe it was their support that saw him through the 1920s and right up to the last farm year. They certainly diffused the tyranny of their step-dad. As Paal got older the thought of his humiliation began to rankle: *he* should have been the boss of the place, not that foul-mouthed intruder. He was treated like any mere hired hand. But to those around him Paal did not act as if he were in a shadow.

He danced with the girls, drank with the fellows, and carried a harmonica in his shirt. They saw him as a charmer, as somebody who was good at enjoying himself. If he chose not to follow through on his dream of leaving, it was more likely because his hatred never exceeded his sense of attachment to the one life he knew. Besides, an avenger had to have patience.

But his mother and step-dad were able to cheat him twice, for in the depression they sold the farm that was his by right and moved east to the town of Hedmark, where they opened a cafe and tavern. Paal concealed his bitterness and tagged along, though times being as they were he couldn't have done much else. In Hedmark he had a job tending bar, that was something; and after awhile his mother even handed over the remains of his patrimony, a thousand dollars, that was really something. Maybe he should have returned to the Sheyenne and used it to get a piece of his farm back. Hell, he knew what all he *should* have done. At the moment that he decided to have a peek at the world instead, go to Minneapolis and shoot the whole wad on women, drinks and hotels, at that mad moment he didn't care if he saw the Sheyenne valley ever again.

He had met some deep-thinking people too in Minneapolis, and when he showed up broke at the cafe and tavern, having ridden the rods, Paal's mind was afire. Ma put him to work behind the bar again; the customers had always liked talking to him. But now if they complained about the lack of jobs or money, he had the words to set them straight. They were living through the demise of capitalism, this so-called depression was created by the boozhwazee in order to enslave the workers, they better hurry up and seize the means of production, and any day an American Hitler was bound to arise. Paal's easy manner took the edge off his evangelizing and he enjoyed the long arguments he got into. The only instant converts were two bachelor brothers from town who had once been in the Socialist party. Everyone else was content to wrangle and have another draft. Paal didn't worry; those guys in the cities had said it would take time. But what kept him at it was the effect all this had on his mother. She may have been able to reconcile Christianity with the selling of beer, yet Paal's reasoned atheism she took as an offense. Even after she quit debating him she had to put up with his gibes. He would approach, Good Book in hand, telling her that she *mustn't forget her daily opium.*

It was in Hedmark that he got to know Ida. The Iversons were living then in a shack at one corner of town, and the lawyer did more card playing than anything else, but there were a couple of fairly good-looking daughters in his brood. Paal had seen her around and heard that she used to work as a maid in Fargo but had gone to study to be a teacher; he first met and talked to her at a dance in Abercrombie. (Just because he had joined the workers of the world it didn't mean he couldn't still have fun.) They seemed to get along well enough, he and Ida, though she was a bit shy and awkward and unlike some of those better-off girls who were quick to pull a man into the hay. Oh he liked her as she was, and he knew that she appreciated his own qualities. This was the big thing. They started going out, more or less, in the summer of 1940 when Paal was thirty-one and Ida, with her curled brown hair and solemn white face, in her middle twenties. On a night too warm for dancing they took a stroll along the Milwaukee tracks and he sang her the tune Slim Yim and the Rockets had made so popular.

> *I asked her Papa for her hand in marriage*
> *and got the answer in the strangest way:*
> *I never yet have left from any doorway*
> *in such a hurry as I did that day.*
>
> *Then I went home and wrote to Nikolina:*
> *"Oh, Nikolina, won't you meet me soon;*
> *meet me in the woods on Wednesday evening*
> *and be there with the rising of the moon."*

They returned hand in hand, both knowing, without having said a word out of the ordinary, that something momentous had begun.

Ida's father was not like Nikolina's, he cared only about whist and the political situation. But old lady Iverson sensed it right away and scolded her daughter for being seen with a no-good who was an atheist on top of it. This hurt Ida more than Paal, who having survived under a shadow since the age of ten was merely amused at people's small-mindedness. Ya they might call him a low-lifer and a radical, but what did the Iversons have to boast of? Ida got a job that fall at a country school near Wahpeton and they were both just as glad; with her away from home they could court in peace.

That fall too his folks' cafe and tavern burned down. Ma took it as God's judgment and fell to her knees and was saved for the third time. Even his gentile step-dad suddenly got religion. Paal figured it was either sparks from the locomotive, or one of the Iverson kids, whom he had thrown out of the bar earlier, that started it. Whatever the cause, the effect was they had no place to live and no source of income. They did have a few dollars and a car that worked, so the folks decided to hit the road. Being Norwegian-born, they were a mind to go west and see salt water again; Paal could jump in or follow as he chose. The two brothers nearest him in age were already making a career of the army and three sisters had also left the nest. He hesitated long enough to receive a blessing and a ten-dollar bill from Ma, then stood grinning as he watched the folks and all his half-siblings trundle away on the straight dry road to Oregon.

He'd think of a way to get by till next spring, then he could always hire out to some local farm. He knew he had a stake in this prairie and he didn't want to leave her.

Paal did have to ride the rods to Minneapolis, though, where luckily he got night work pushing broom. The site of his one great splurge seemed drearier than it had and the thought of checking in with his old Communist buddies was depressing. He spent his days just looking around that blame jungle, and if his feet got too sore he'd hum a tune for consolotation.

> *When you're in love, you're in awful torture —*
> *whoever's tried it will not disagree:*
> *I was so very fond of Nikolina*
> *and Nikolina just as fond of me.*

Ida's letters told a no happier story. North Dakota in the winter was a place to make anyone lonesome; being among strangers there was almost more than she could handle. She stayed at a farmhouse in a cell-sized room, got up in the black of morning and walked a chilly mile to build a fire in the school stove, then bore with the dumbest kids she had ever seen until the sun fell into the west like an exhausted hope. Week after week, the same ordeal. Oh, she'd gone to Hedmark twice but hadn't dared say anything further to Mama, who would never, never approve of them — so why even bother to mention it? But Ida would assure him, in her pure and simple penmanship, that not *every* hope was tired. It was just that the two of them might have to keep their intentions to themselves.

When she resigned in January and came down on a bus, that was all right with Paal. So was the marriage. They didn't have a lot to give each other. The room they honeymooned in was not much better than the one she had left. As to what they'd do next or where they'd do it, neither could say. But while people were getting shot to bits in Europe and China and all over the globe, he and Ida were at least together and among the living. He didn't mind a balding hand towel or a smelly rug or the sound of a man choking on his vomit in the hall; if this was rock bottom he couldn't complain. They had health and happiness and in this cold-blooded world you didn't need more than that.

But in spring, Ida expecting, they quit Minneapolis without regret. Soon they were back in North Dakota and on the good side of old lady Iverson, though they had to make her a grandmother before she'd let them in the house. Lacking a car and a welcome, they had stayed in Fargo where Paal managed to win their bread as a part-time laborer at various stores and shipping companies and Ida looked after herself and wrote daily letters to Hedmark. Peter and Pearl Harbor and Christmas at the Iversons' and Ida's bout with scarlet fever came all inside of two months, but Paal stood up well under the changes. Once Ida recovered, she and the baby were often out at the eastern estate and this meant a load off his back. He'd been missing work on account of pains in it; he figured it was those heavy unloading jobs had done him in; and if *he* didn't watch himself, nobody would. Now that Ida and Peter had free board and room he could take a home cure.

He wasn't sad to say goodbye to Fargo, either, when they decided to move in with the Iversons as the spring fieldwork was beginning. That season there were no hired hands to spare and Paal could work about wherever he liked, so throughout the quiet summer of 1942 he rode tractor at a neighboring farm. It was nice to be able to chip in on the food and that Ida had help with Peter; however they both thought it was even nicer just being in the country. The wheat grew tall and the cottonwood leaves thick under a dependable sun. Paal relished this time, hoping it would somehow continue. The seasonal work should bring in enough to get them through the winters. But radio and newspaper agreed that there was a war on, and the organization which had carried away the young men who would have been competing for his job might also summon Paal. If the generals wanted him they'd have to start hunting in Valley City, then the notice would be forwarded to Ma's Hedmark address and on to Oregon, and she hadn't gotten it or she would have written. He thought he'd be wise to do nothing — not that he was afraid, he simply didn't want to be bothered. Ida said that he should try for a deferment. O.H. Iverson told him it was his duty to enlist. According to Jensine, people were talking about him. So with a shrug Paal went to turn himself in.

They were sure hustling along at the induction center; it was like they were afraid to give you a chance to think twice. He had no trouble with the written exam and sensed he was going to pass the physical too, so he stepped bare naked out of the line of recruits and told that army sawbones about it. The doctor poked around and finally said he was missing a disc. Paul was 4-F. On the home jaunt he did a lot of reflecting. See what could happen if you didn't speak up for yourself sometimes! He'd had no back pains all summer, and fieldwork wasn't light, but you never knew. At other times it didn't hurt to keep your mouth shut.

They hung on one more year at the eastern estate, then Ida got itchy to move. She wanted to join her relatives in their Seattle adventure, and Paal, weary of O.H. Iverson and the carping Jensine, felt up to travel again. Peter was older too. They boarded a bus with high expectations, arrived the same way, and soon got situated in a government housing project. Ida seemed to love that soggy town with its fog and traffic, but Paal hated it. He was sucked into a routine such as he had never imagined, mornings out into the wet cold to squeeze himself onto a trolley, punching a clock, days sweating in the engine room of some greasy Russian ship, punching a clock, riding a trolley, evenings spent on the couch, nights he couldn't remember, and only further dark mornings ahead. Weekends he stayed in like a convalescent. Why mill with the mob unless you have to? As Bee said, "Here you're just another face at the checkout counter." If Ida didn't suffer it was because she had relatives to visit with and the kid for entertainment. But his was a dog's lot. No wonder his back started acting up; often the pain was so bad he couldn't go to work. In the spring of '45 he missed two weeks in a row. At first Ida went easy on him, applying the hot towels and everything, but then Oliver Iverson called him a shirker and she got nervous. They had a hell of a fight, the two of them, Ida screaming, Paal breaking a mop handle over his knee. Oh that passed when he returned to the yards; his raise helped too. But he and Ida hadn't acted like this before, not in North Dakota.

The whipping of the Japs made people laugh and dance like fools, but the skies were as gray as ever. It was a chore to carry Peter to General Doolittle's parade, holding an umbrella in a field of umbrellas as the crowd shouted welcome and the wind hissed; fine there should be heroes and that the kid should get to see one, but Monday morning Paal would have to go back to the yards anyhow. The layoff scare in September gave him hope. He couldn't understand why the other men were so worried about losing their jobs. It was then also that the Iversons finally came up with an idea he liked: to move home. One afternoon a union boss talked to all the guys on his shift and announced that every other worker might soon be cut, and if anybody had been planning to leave he should do it now so as to give the rest a better chance, and those choosing voluntary layoff would not be quitting, hence they'd be eligible for unemployment compensation. The steward privately assured him of a job, but Paal said thanks, his wife was determined to go home to North Dakota and that was that. When he boarded the trolley for that last damn time he had a beer in his lunchkit, good news — omitting some details — for Ida and much to look forward to.

Bee and Lester owned one more car than they needed (Lester used to pick up junked autos to tinker with), and Paal got the coupe for thirty-six bucks. Seattle, Washington, to Fargo, North Dakota, is quite a drive but the Pontiac seemed eager to make it; he really had to watch the footfeed. Those clouds were traveling right behind them. They arrived in the valley at nightfall, yet to somebody who had escaped worse darkness it was like a perfect dawning.

Ever since the return Paal had been easy in his mind. In North Dakota you could breathe for nothing, by God, and there was a good mile between you and the next fellow, and though the place wasn't much on scenery, it *knew* you and you knew it, so no matter what happened to you here you'd be able to work things out. He wished Ida could relax more. Ya they should have a home, but they could just as well sit at the eastern estate for the time being, at least until his unemployment came through, then it would be spring and he could get fieldwork. No use telling her what he thought; Ida wanted them to be on their own, period, and once she had a notion fixed in her brain it didn't help to argue. Better pretending to go along with her, driving up to Fargo and making an apparent effort to do the necessary things. The one real necessary thing was keeping her happy. They would not live in Fargo and he would not punch a time clock again, he'd see to that, by God, and if Ida's plans didn't turn out the way she expected maybe she'd *have* to learn to enjoy life. He'd see that she never blamed him, at any rate. She would be content in the end and none the wiser.

Therefore a Pontiac coupe sat gathering sun near the Amidon Bar.

He had drunk here in their Fargo days, when it had been a pretty wild joint, but now the older guys had moved in and it was quiet except for the radio. *A year ago he was the only senator who voted against* the extension of lend-lease, and as Langer explained.... The news went through him faster than the beer; this Milwaukee stuff was not like the rain water they served you in Seattle and you had to nurse it. He took each slow sip as a pleasure hard-earned.

After he and another fellow, a couple of stools down, had been sitting there long enough to establish a presence, they got to talking about the weather and the economy. The man was a farmer of middle age and perhaps a German — he didn't catch the *norsk* phrases Paal threw out.

The war may have been over but life's troubles were not. If it came too little rain next spring, or if your farm equipment went haywire, or if the price of wheat declined and everything you had to buy shot up, or say if a man got bedridden, you didn't know *what* you'd do. Both agreed that the world is a vale of tears.

Paal's was a tragic story: "Ya, I was at the shipyards and after V-J Day they were in one *hell* of a hurry to get me out of there. I had a handicap too, what you call for a spine injury, but a family man has to work so I was doing the best I could. You think they'd have a heart? Nossir! They just handed me my walking papers and showed me the door, and not a job to be had in that whole stinking town. We decided to give it a try back here again, and what do I find? The same identical mess. If we don't freeze or starve to death we'll be lucky, that's all I can say."

He had forgotten his Communism in the hold of a Russian ship.

The farmer looked as though he had been eating regularly during the war, but still he could sympathize. Last year at harvest his gas tractor had broken down and he'd had to try the old steam engine, and as he struggled to get it running he had a terrible pain in his side, so his wife took him to the hospital and they kept him for an operation. That ruptured appendix cost him a year's work, and all because of no tractor parts on the market; therefore he too had known suffering.

Paal nodded, once to him, once to the barkeep. The war hit everybody. "Now you can find the parts but you sure gotta pay," he said.

They drank in thinking silence, waiting for someone to come up with an idea. It was the farmer.

"You're needing a place to live, you say. Well I have a brother farming south of town and he's got a vacant house. I wonder, though; there hasn't been people in it since those Mexicans, it's more of a shanty, and I don't know how it heats. I suppose you could drive out and see for yourself. It's no mansion, I warn you. But he wouldn't go too high on the rent."

Paal let himself be convinced. If he had two addresses instead of one to show Ida, the news of the failed job interview might be easier to bear; and why not humor the man? Paal said he was in a bind so he couldn't very well seem indifferent. What he got was not an address but a road map in pencil. He could easily stop there on the way to Hedmark.

But he thought he would wait. Ida'd prefer to live in town.

He was about ready for the taste of snoose and a slow afternoon drive when he heard something he never liked to hear. The drunken voice of his brother-in-law was unmistakable.

"Hey Paal, what do you know!"

The youngest of the Iverson litter had gotten out of uniform early and joined the others in Seattle where he had gone alcoholic. They didn't seem to know why the army had railroaded him, and nobody discussed it, but Paal had always thought this was the guy who had fired the cafe and tavern so he wasn't surprised. Now he had moved his drinking enterprises back to North Dakota.

Lyle mounted a stool between Paal and the German. He was a short pink man with thinning yellow hair.

"I saw your jalopy in front and I says to myself, I says, I'm going in and have a talk with Paal!"

"Oh is that right."

"Lemme tell you Paal, you haven't amounted to anything but I think there's hope yet."

Paal considered giving him a tap on the jaw but there were too many watchers. If you didn't maintain a friendly distance, a sonofabitch like this could get you in trouble; so Paal kept smiling.

"Is that right. I hoped you were going to tell me about your army career."

"Shit," said Lyle. He was distracted by the appearing of the bartender. "I gotta have a drink. Buy me a drink, Paal! Where's the goddamn can? Buy me a drink and when I come back from the goddamn can I'm having a talk with you."

As Lyle swayed off into the recesses, Paal excused himself. "No sale," he said to the barkeep. He thanked the farmer and directed a casual parting remark at the both of them:

"I guess I'll just leave him in his own shit."

It had turned cloudy during his hours in the Amidon but the clouds were passing and again it was weather to reflect a quiet mind. However, as Paal drove south he was sucking his wad in a rage. The worst of a rotten·bunch, that Lyle! A sot and a firebug and only the Iversons were dumb enough to put up with him — the army sure wasn't. Paal hated the family he had married into; their smugness and their belittling comments were more than a man could stand. It was time to set Ida straight. Either you say goodbye to Mama or I'm going it alone! She can just have her damn family and see how much she likes it. And if that sonfoabitching brother of hers ever crosses my path there'll be all hell to pay!

Outside of town there was nothing to limit the spread of sky over half of creation. A Pontiac moved on the Red River valley, the other half. Then it left the main road.

He studied the map which the German had drawn for him. It was less than a mile to the river. He might as well have a look at this grand shanty. Paal wanted to avoid the eastern estate. He had seen plenty Iversons for one day.

III. A Dumb Toy

They lit the kerosene lamps and ate at the round table in the living room, Papa first, of course, green tea and biscuits and salt pork, and after he had gone back to his rocking chair Mama set out corn and meatballs and fried potatoes for Ida and the child. Jensine usually stayed in the kitchen, eating and cleaning up at the same time. She had fixed supper for three but one had not arrived, so there'd be leftovers to keep warm.

"*Hei sa'n!*" Papa marched to the kitchen. He must have forgotten his evening toothpick. He also must have forgotten that he and Jensine didn't converse directly, because now he made a statement while alone in the room with her.

"Villiam Verner is going places!"

He even waited, as though expecting a reply. There was silence in the kitchen, but Mama's hostility followed him out.

Sitting in his rocker again, he had a toothpick to help him ruminate. "He'll do awright, that young fellow," he continued, unabashed. "He's got education and he's not scared of vork. Ideas are fine but they're not enough in politics. You got to have ambition too! William Verner has vhat it takes! So, Ida, vhere's that husband of yours?"

She had been concentrating on Peter and the food, not letting things affect their little ceremony. Peter didn't really need to be watched, he ate gladly and a lot, and she knew who he got that from. Strange that Paal was late; he enjoyed his meals.

Ida looked up but not at her father. "I suppose maybe he had a flat or something," she said.

"If a man is married he ought to discharge his responsibilities. But Paal Malmlund doesn't have vhat it takes."

She was done, and Peter almost. They could just as well move to the kitchen. There were so many better things to do, the dishes for instance, than listening to Papa; he didn't want you to answer anyway, figured you didn't have a mind to speak.

O.H. Iverson was left rocking, his mouth still open, but showed no distress. A heap of newspapers and detective magazines lay at his elbow.

The radio stood within reach. Womenfolks had their place and he had his.

Safely with Mama, she could smile and tell Peter how good he had been. He got a chocolate drop cookie for dessert. Then there was water to be carried from the rain barrel and stoking the range to heat it. Having electricity and running water in Seattle may have spoiled her, but Ida didn't mind hefting the old pail again, not tonight.

Peter was driving a yellow toy tractor on the fields of the floor, and now Mama was smiling too. That toy had been the gift of Alvin, her childless brother, and whatever Alvin gave was really special, if only because it came from him. Peter's activity seemed like a tribute.

The floor was worn rough. Ida told him not to get a sliver in his hand.

"You needn't wash the kettle, I stuck the potatoes and meatballs in there," said Mama.

Someone had turned on the radio: — *York and Washington. Stay tuned now for boxing.* And right on the hour the living room clock began striking seven.

Peter ran to the north window as though impelled by the sounds of the house.

"Is Daddy here?"

She joined him and peeked into the darkness, though not quite seriously. She had just been out to the barrel and if there were a car approaching she'd know it. But then she heard a clank and a rattle and saw a single dim orange headlamp bobbing across the yard.

"Well I guess he's back," she said.

Mama got up from her stool and slid the kettle of leftovers to the center of the range. In the next room the din of a boxing match went on. Peter steered his tractor toward the noises.

"I broke a fanbelt," said Paal with a small shy grin. "I was outside Hickson when I heard the snap. Lucky there was a garage open in town."

As he ate he told the story of his good day, talking like a successful hunter. Ida had noticed the scent of beer on him. That was all right; beer meant he'd be cheerful. He sure is handsome, she thought.

But someone had switched off the radio and all that could be heard was Peter's imitation of a tractor engine until the rocking chair creaked and weighty footsteps were nearing.

"How goes it, Paal — have you been vasting your life?" said O.H. Iverson.

"Noo, I don't think you could say that." Paal ignored the sarcasm.

Ida saw that under his grin there wasn't the cheerfulness she had imagined. Anger showed in the way he bit his food.

"I spose it's getting cold out there," said Mama.

"Oh you can tell it's fall."

But O.H. Iverson wasn't to be diverted. His blue eyes shone with fun and malice. "You knaw, if a man is going to do anything in this vorld he has to set his shoulder to the *vheel*. He can't bum around depending on others. Here you have a vife and kid, and vhat consideration do you give to them? You better get on the *stick*, Paal."

"Thank you for the advice." Paal's tone was bland. However, Ida realized that a black spell was coming.

"Vell vhat you got to say for yourself!"

Paal slammed down his fork. His voice was shaking but the small grin remained. "Now you listen here, Mister Attorney. I do what I can the best I can and I answer to nobody. Understand? And how is it you're the great one to talk, who never cared a damn for your own wife and kids? How bout the time you threw Ida's doll in the stove, tell me that."

Oh, no! thought Ida.

"Vell, as far as I'm concerned you can just get out!"

Paal did so, charging into the raw October night in shirtsleeves. His foot bumped some object, maybe the kid's wagon, and he gave it a kick to remember. Sonofabitching Iversons! Tomorrow he'd be out of here and tomorrow couldn't come soon enough! Thank God he had done what he'd done. Paal circled the car and circled the car, feeling the still warm breath of the radiator on each pass, but he did not get in.

Ida went running out after Paal.

O.H.'s expression had changed; he looked almost stupified. *"Nei* vhat did he mean? That *I* threw Ida's doll in the stove? I never threw Ida's doll in the stove."

Twice this evening he had ignored the ban on conversations with Jensine. He recollected himself and started for the living room, but he was too late.

"Ya they can well make trouble for their kids that didn't make money to feed them."

Jensine's words hit the back of his head like shattering glass. The radio stayed silent. The rocker was creaking again. Peter took his toy to the north window.

"Where are they going?"

"Oh they're just gonna sit out in the car talking awhile," said Jensine, her tone once more a grandmother's. "They'll be in pretty soon. You have another cookie."

But Ida had to walk with him until he cooled off. Over and over they trod the driveway and the near stretch of the township road in the moonlessness. The air felt like winter. There was hardly a wind; what little blew, blew no earth smells. It would freeze by morning.

She knew better than to interrupt Paal's monologue, which also kept covering the same ground. "Nobody talks to me like that! You visit the in-laws a few days and expect civil treatment and what do you get? Well I can put up with many things but this I won't put up with. I'm just going down that road tonight and your loving father can deliver you and the kid and all our junk when I'm damn good and ready, so piss on it!"

Ida remembered the doll-burning. She was perhaps five at the time; yes, her brother Jim was the baby. Papa was working at his desk and she had been warned not to go in there, but the doll — what had she called her? — looked so nice in the pink dress Mama had sewn that she couldn't resist showing him. Papa grabbed the doll with a shout and tossed her in the round oak stove. Ida screamed, out of fear, not sorrow, as the iron door closed on the thing she loved. That first pure experience of pain had never since been equalled, hence it was unforgotten. She had told Paal of it and he hadn't forgotten either. It was odd he brought it up, an incident she had spoken of only once, but not that Papa himself couldn't remember it.

"And what kind of person would do that to his own daughter? He thinks he can criticize *me?*"

"Oh he put that doll out of his mind the minute it happened," Ida said.

They were in the car now. Paal had opened his snoose can — a sign of recuperation. The chilliest of the air couldn't touch them; this tight familiar space was all theirs. They had sat within it and seen the ridges of Washington go by. In Idaho and Montana they had been happy right here.

Paal had more to say: "Hell, I can get along with anybody. People have troubles enough in this life, so I don't bother them and they don't bother me. If they step out of line I set them straight; otherwise I live and let live. That's the only way to do things. That's why it went so good up in Fargo. I had no trouble *what*soever. As long as Mister O.H. Iverson behaves himself I can be just as nice as you please, but if he comes dictating to me, then look out."

He rolled down the window, briefly, to spit.

Ida felt the warmth of his hand on her knee. This freed her mournfulness. "I don't know, Paal. Sometimes I wish we could get along with my family better. I can't imagine being without them, they mean so much. Oh I don't say they're perfect, they're no different from others, they can act thougthlessly, just like Papa and that doll — he wasn't *trying* to hurt me, he simply got carried away, now he doesn't even remember. And who cares about a dumb toy? If only we didn't need them, then I spose we could pack our bags and leave. But we *do* have responsibilities, Paal, what with Peter and finding a home and a job and all the rest. Here I was so *glad* to have the war over and everyone back in the valley, but now I just don't know!"

She ended in tears.

"Don't worry about all that stuff," he said. "You and me are going up to Fargo in the morning and we're gonna find a place, I bet you. I got the arrangements worked out in my head, so you relax and enjoy yourself. We have each other and a healthy son and this here old car and what else can we ask."

He had spoken kindly but his hand wasn't there anymore.

They waited in a careful silence. Best be easy on the girl, Paal was thinking, she gets a little confused. She still can't look objective at her damn fool father and see what he is, but once out of here she'll understand. He was pleased he'd taken the chance he had today. He could always tell her the whole deal, but no point in that; it would only upset her. Best let the girl have it one thing at a time.

Ida was thinking that she really wanted to believe him, and how wonderful if the room in Fargo were as nice as he said, and the place outside of town, but she knew Paal's talent for acting. His description of the job interview seemed too, too familiar. Earnest Paal goes in to apply, hard-hearted manager turns him down. Had she heard that story ten times or a hundred, ye gods! He'd spent money on beer too, and she doubted fanbelts were cheap. Well there was no choice but ride along and hope, and maybe have a little session with God. Poor Paal wanted nothing to do with Him either.

Ya he had the whole of tomorrow mapped out; now he could quit figuring. Paal took a deep breath and stretched, yawning as he exhaled.

"We're gonna have a busy day," he said.

"I spose we could take our lunch then."

"That might be an idea. I had another idea too. Think Jensine would mind if we got in late?"

"You mean in the evening?"

"Ya I saw where they're playing 'The Lost Weekend' at the Roxy, you know."

"She just loves having Peter."

"So I thought we could go to a show, that might be fun."

"Well if we can afford it, I guess. Peter likes being out here. He wouldn't complain."

Light lowered in the thin-curtained windows of the front room, then disappeared altogether. In a couple of minutes a door thumped. Ida couldn't see back of the house but she knew that her father was making his last night offering to the earth. The door sprang shut again. She pictured him climbing the stairs, the candle in its saucer held high, a lonely man on the way to sleep; and soon there was a glimmering in the dormer window as he passed through to the south room. The kitchen lamp was still on but Mama would be getting ready, banking up the coals for tomorrow and having a goodnight sip of coffee with sugar and milk, a tireless woman at her day's end; in a while she and Peter would be going to the outhouse. Ida wasn't surprised to hear the door a third time. The glint from Mama's kerosene lantern appeared on the wall of the shed. No more was visible.

"I better get in," said Ida, "Peter should be put to bed."

"Everybody's hitting the sack, it looks like." Paal tried to sound disinterested. *"Jeg ska sover i bilen da.* I should be comfortable out here. Was there a blanket I could use?"

"Oh I bet he's already forgotten what he said, and you. Just come on in. You'd freeze in the car."

"Let's sit a little bit longer then."

Ida smiled at her husband.

Finally, hand in hand, they crossed the patch of yard to retire with the eastern estate.

IV. Weather Change

The morning, another clear one, sped them away. As they pitched onto the bright gravel road, engine roaring, Mama and Peter waving, it was more like the start of an adventure than a day trip. The car forged north as if the valley were a sea and their destination some unvisited shore; the dust waked out astern. In all the plowing or stubble of the Indian summer landscape there was no one and nothing, not even a bird, to stop them. They could just sail on. Both felt the tugging of the distances and they talked of many an earlier voyage, Minneapolis to Fargo, Fargo to Seattle, Seattle home, knowing and not saying that this was still part of their most recent — they had yet to anchor. But, young in a young day, they didn't lack for hope.

"I got a hunch we're on the right track," said Paal.

His cheeks were slick from the razor. He had shaved in front of Papa's mirror, and Papa had seen him, but the two men had acted fine.

Ida beamed in the ring of a wool scarf. Mama had insisted she wear it, also a heavy brown coat; if you got a chill, no telling what it'd lead to. At her side she had Paal's old lunchkit, the contents of which would take them into the evening.

"What a simply *glorious* time to be traveling," she said. "I almost wish — —"

But soon, too soon. billboards and houses were accumulating on either side and there were great bare elms overhead. Fargo wasn't a tall town so you never saw it approaching; you were just into it. Suddenly you had to quit your wayfaring dreams and muster your wits.

Having lost the envelope with the address on it, Paal couldn't find the place immediately; off north Broadway, he said he thought. This was the kind of thing that always tensed him up, and Ida marveled at his calmness. They got there rather late.

The woman seemed not to mind, however, showing them in with a few cordial remarks and ignoring Paal's timid look. He had been ready to duck the blow of her eyes, "So there was a wife all along, you bastard!" and to turn her pique to advantage. They couldn't well rent a room from someone like that, could they? He hadn't worn the wedding band, so that wasn't it. Maybe he had talked too much. Whatever it was she had, she'd certainly gotten over it quick!

"As I was telling your husband, I can supply the linen and the soap and towels."

"Ah," said Ida politely.

She was warming to the house, and to its owner. The room was neat though not forbiddingly spotless, same for the bath; they'd feel at home here. Once Peter got a cot or a rollaway they wouldn't need to buy any more furniture, and there was ample drawer and closet space. She sure had to give Paal credit this time.

"I spose Peter could sleep over there then," Ida thought aloud, pointing to a vacant area by the south window.

"Oh you have a child?"

Paal saw that the woman was a bit confused and he jumped in with a grin. "Ya, he's going on four and a regular demon, let me tell you, but you know little boys."

"Uff-da what a thing to say!" Ida laughed at what she took to be a joke, but had they been at the estate she would have reproached him. And wasn't it just like him to forget to mention Peter?

The woman laughed too, and there went her doubts. "Well, I'm not used to children, I never had any of my own, but if he's as nice as his parents —"

"He's no problem at all, believe me," said Ida.

Paal hid his annoyance. It was bad enough to have misjudged this widow, worse that she hadn't misjudged him. Now they were exchanging compliments, Ida thanking her for holding the room when there was such a terrible demand, the woman replying that it was better to wait and have good tenants than to hurry, and Paal chewed his lip. There had to be a way of stopping this nonsense and getting out for a touch of snooze.

"I'm asking twelve dollars a month," the woman said in conclusion.

Ida had feared it would be twenty, and her heart missed a beat. They could have the room for a nod! They'd want a house eventually but for the moment they couldn't hope to do better. Having a place to move in to would rid her of the instant worries, then she could think about Paal and the job situation and so forth.

"That's pretty reasonable, I guess," she said cautiously. "We should be able to manage twelve all right."

But there was a line of concern on Paal's forehead. He looked at her and at the landlady as though they were both strangers. "As I say, it's ideal and all that but we may not be able to pay the rent regular. I'm trying to find work only I got this bad back, you see, and the future's kind of uncertain."

Rage took hold of Ida. What in *heaven's* name was wrong with him? She didn't dare glance at the other woman. She turned to Paal with affected nonchalance.

"There's the unemployment compensation, remember."

"Well that's kind of in limbo too." His half whisper indicated that this was a private affair.

The lady of the house had greeted them in a print dress and lipstick. It wasn't her appearance but her manner that was no longer so hospitable. Maybe she had begun to share Paal's concern. After a decent interval, she said:

"I've been in financial difficulties myself so I can sympathize, and I'd still like to rent to you. Suppose I had to ask for six months' in advance, how would that be?"

Ida didn't bother to compute the sum; she realized it would gobble up most of the eighty-four dollars they had saved and that Paal, who was shaking his head in triumph, realized it too. What had gotten into him was beyond her. Further bargaining would be pointless. She told the woman that six months' rent was more than they could handle, thanked her, tightened the scarf-knot under her chin and walked to the door.

"I'm very sorry it didn't work out," she heard the woman say.

Paal sounded happy at last: "So are we! Pleasure to meet you now! Hope you get some good folks in!"

She was already sitting in the car. He saw her rigid profile and knew that the next hour wasn't gonna be easy. Ida had one hell of a temper. This would be the tough part; get by the next hour and he'd have clear sailing again.

He hopped in and hit the switch and the Pontiac rolled. "Well so much for her," he said with a chuckle. "You know, I had a feeling we wouldn't take that room, and then she wanted all our money on top of it. Ha! Oh I understand you're peeved and that I can understand, but don't just go blowing your stack. I got a much, much nicer place to show you."

Sunlight flashed on the lid of Paal's snoose can. Ida was immune and unmoving, her jaw outthrust, her arms clenched. To him she had one thing only to say:

"Don't you *ever* pull another stunt like that."

The almost shiny Pontiac began a further exploration of northside Fargo, turning at every other intersection and making tentative stops here and there. Both driver and passenger were silent.

He had thought it best to let Ida alone, but his quiet cruising would remind her that something needed to be said. Finally he gave in:

"We were sposed to go to Bee?"

Lester and Bee lived north of Front Street, that's all he knew; the address had been on that damn lost envelope. Now Ida had wanted to see them and she could remember stuff like addresses and a sisterly chat might do her good, so it was up to her to speak. But his sheepish tone had no effect on Ida.

Downtown, like most of Fargo, is some yards higher than the Red. Broadway crosses Front Street in the middle of the district, then drops south to end at Island Park. This is low ground, near the river and in spring at its mercy. But it was during a spring flood that the hill here gave the park a name. It's more mound than hill, yet the trees and the grass and the squirrels have been in charge so long that the park does seem insular. Humanity washes around. The King of Norway brought quite a wave to the pavilion in 1939; however, people usually stay out. June Sundays, a family of Mexican beet workers might loll and picnic in the shade, and at other tepid times you might see an old stray derelict or a couple with children in tow, and these are the exceptions. After the leaves fall and the benches disappear, you won't find even them, not even on the shores of the park. This October island is for statues only.

He sat humbly with his lunchkit under the stare of an elevated stone soldier. He had noticed but not read the words on the plinth: *In Memory Of Our Comrades, 1861 - 1865*. The resting sod felt warm. It was, as he had suggested, a good spot to have lunch. He was also in view of the Pontiac and took care not to look that way. He didn't raise his head at all, just kept it hanging as would befit a soul in trouble; to behave natural would infuriate Ida.

Here I am between two statues, Paal thought. He was hungry and he had the food and he mustn't touch it.

The sun had begun to edge out of its highest point. Fat squirrels were running and arguing through messes of dead leaves, and now and then the last fly of the year would buzz him. He ignored all this too.

Ida was glad to have a moment to herself. Had he really *wanted* to make fools of them? Why so much bother for something small and nasty like that? She could stand the embarrassment, what she couldn't bear was the idea that he had *wanted* it. Perhaps he was trying to be funny. If so, the joke was beyond her for one. Ida rehearsed the sequence in her mind: Paal sees room, makes appointment; Paal and I go to inspect; I like room, landlady seems to like us; Paal sabotages the whole thing. It simply didn't hold together, not unless she assumed that Paal had had no intention of going through with it in the first place. But why didn't he say so? Why drag her along? He hadn't even offered to explain, just tittered like a kid. If he could think of nothing but pranks, and his family without house and desperate, then he was not the man he claimed to be. "Don't blow your stack," ye gods! No now she'd have to do some reconsidering, and she could use more than a moment to herself. Had she been able to drive, she would have up and left him at his dirty little picnic.

She sat until the fuming subsided, then untightened her arms. The windows were up and the air stank of gas. Paal moped in the offing. He had on a clean white shirt; she had ironed it after breakfast. But he was one miserable sight, by golly. Her breathing had slowed. Can't lay around forever, she thought, too much to do.

Paal himself had been figuring on what to do next — rather, how to go about it. She might be stubborn enough to refuse to look at the shanty. He could drive her there without a word, a glimpse of it'd make her feel better, or if the time didn't seem right they could head back to the farm. She wouldn't like returning emptyhanded, though, so he'd have to tell her.

He was pleased to see her ambling across the lawn. The earth under his rump was getting harder.

Ida stopped awhile to scan the monument. "I think it's laudable," she said as though to no one in particular, "to honor the brave men who did their duty and gave their lives for the nation."

The scarf and winter coat put some age on her; but for that, she might have been any young wife on any pleasant day's outing. She came up to him as she would have approached someone she hadn't met, though not with the routine smile. Paal was hangdog as ever. She stood at a polite distance.

"We should have had a sandwich at least." She sounded weary, not mad.

Paal got to his feet like an invalid, stretched and nodded. His glossy black hair was in disorder.

"Ya that's true," he said, almost whimpering. "Might as well crank up the buggy then."

"Shouldn't we eat here?"

"Well ya, but."

They avoided each other's eyes. Both the ground and the trees seemed more interesting. A wind rushed through the naked branches, and Paal slipped into his jacket again.

"It's getting colder too," he said.

"Or did you have something in mind?"

"How about we go to that place south of town and have a bite there?"

Paal regained his spirits as the two of them walked slowly to the car. With a parting glance at the scene of his ordeal, he said, "Nothing around here but statues anyway."

His expression was resolute, like that of the Yankee who faced the growing north wind atop the memorial.

In these parts the weather is shifty; quick changes are to be expected in all seasons. A blizzard can choke the roses of June, and it can rain at New Year's. So much is possible. But an extreme change is most likely to occur in fall or spring. One April a dozen retired farmers got heatstruck, while the following October the kids went ice-skating before Halloween. A North Dakotan can only accept what the wind delivers.

They left Fargo accompanied by low hurrying hunks of cloud, and the sun was going off and on like the smile of a crazy person. The wind had no high wheat or barley to blow in, but Indian summer had dried the plowing so it blew dirt. The country was in shadow.

Now we're in for it, Ida was thinking. The weather had been too good to stay. It was as if they were traveling into an ash desert where the farmsteads clung to uncertain earth and nobody could survive out of doors. Soon the sun would be going out forever. The Pontiac had not been tested in real cold; there were sure a lot of drafts. Ida huddled in the coat, blessing Mama for making her wear it.

Soon they were bumping east, Paal wrestling the wheel, in the ruts of what must have been a farm access. He told her it was straight ahead, that there tan building at the end of the field, but they couldn't drive all the way in. They had to park near an empty unattached silo, and once the engine stopped they could hear the wind hooting in the vast cylinder.

It wasn't far, just a hundred-yard sprint along a row of waning fenceposts. They had the breath of the north to hurry them. As they neared, the sun snapped on a couple of times, changing the pale stucco walls to gold. The house sat long and low and blinded in tall dead grass, the weedy slope to the river beginning at its front door. Paal assured Ida it was better than it looked.

Shivering, they reached the leeward side. What was that odor? Ida wrinkled her nose. It was the smell of carrion, ish-da! Must be the remains of an animal or something.

Paal checked the edge of the bank. "Must be something decaying," he said. "It don't come from here though."

"Was the owner sposed to meet us?" said Ida faintly.

"Naw he just gave me the key."

Of course there was trouble with the lock, and Ida waited, her face pinched. Then the door scraped open and they entered a sudden warmth; the afternoon's chill hadn't penetrated. But they found a new odor.

"Don't tell me there's skunks!" she said.

"Oh I wouldn't worry about that." Paal seemed sage and ready to do the talking. "I didn't notice it so much before. I guess one got chased under the house last night. A shanty like this don't have a foundation, you know. It was for summer living, the Mexicanos."

They, the Mexicans no doubt, had thrown quite a farewell party; tin cans and beer bottles covered the floor and the lap of a cushionless sofa that was mostly dust. Skunk wasn't the only smell in here. In these three sordid little rooms there was no toilet. But the Mexicans hadn't cared; the outhouse must have seemed too distant. She hated to think of looking inside the range and the pot-bellied stove. Skunk had obliterated *another* stench, this she could tell from the thousands of mouse droppings. She had counted on electricity and running water too — not on filth like *this*.

God knows she had tried to keep her head up and hope for the best, but now she could feel every part of her sinking, sinking.

"It's pretty bad I'm afraid," she said.

They were still avoiding each other's eyes, but Paal was irrepressible. "Oh it's nothing fancy, it's what you call for a home in the wilds. But we can clean it up in two three days, I'm sure. I'm going out and visit the can and look the place over. You stay in here where it's nice, why don't you."

The east window had grimy panes and a nest of cobwebs. A large gray spider retreated when she came too close. She saw Paal lean into the blast. The outhouse was missing a door and tilted into space at the slope's edge. Down below was the river, hueless and choppy as it toiled against the wind, and over it, in thick woods, a gang of crows had sought refuge. Paal emerged and fixed his belt and started exploring. When he got to the water he stuck one hand in and grinned, waving in her direction — like a clown, she thought.

Ida couldn't believe it all. Did he actually propose to bring his wife and child to live in Mexican squalor? It had to be a joke, his second of the day, and what he had next in store she'd rather not guess.

Soon he was back, hale and ruddy. "I found where we can have a picnic!"

She smiled indulgently. "Oh we'll eat in the car since we'll be leaving anyway."

"We'll have a garden, and I can fish and put up a swing for the kid, and there's berry bushes in the woods. We can do a lot with this place, and at seven dollars a month we're not gonna go broke either."

Paal's enthusiasm seemed so unlike him, yet she knew it was real. He wasn't being funny. He *did* mean it. As for her, she meant to avert a certain horrid suspicion and get out now.

"That's it, I've seen enough," she said.

There was a pause as he scratched his ear and the seat of his pants. He no longer resembled the brave Yankee. Uneasily, and again in a whimper, he spoke the words:

"Ya but I already paid and took it."

Ida seemed imperturbable. She strolled into the south room as though to have another look. However, when she returned there was a beer bottle in her hand. It whistled past him and cracked against the wall. Then she was shouting.

"So you've been playing a game, have you? Think you can lead me by the nose, hah? Expect your wife and child to live in shit and be glad of it, is that right! Well I've had my fill! You're just a mealy-mouthed conniver! I've seen enough, I said, enough of this dump and enough of you!"

How she got to the car she didn't know. Her head, no her entire body, was in eruption. Her panting wouldn't cease. He was to take her to the estate and pack his bags and go, that much she remembered saying.

The lunchkit sat unopened. Only this morning she had prepared it, love and trust in her heart, and only this morning that same fool heart had ridden the seas with joy. She yanked up the lid. The sandwiches were a pain to behold. The bread had come from Mama, the summer sausage from Uncle Alvin, there was good strong coffee in the thermos; and all for what? Jerking herself out of the car, she tore the sandwiches in bits and scattered them over the dark plowing.

As Paal crept along, he saw his thermos jug bounce off the silo.

Ida baffled him. He had thought the house would be such a pleasant surprise, two months' rent paid and nothing to do but move in, that she'd want to celebrate and go to a show; he had planned the whole thing. But now she was in a fury and threatening to railroad him. Paal was stunned.

He got into the driver's seat, licked his lips and blinked. A lot of dirt in that wind, he thought he should say, but he merely coughed and went on licking and blinking. Ida was hunched at the other door, as far away as she could get, no use to speak to her. Still, he had to try.

"Well I spose I should apologize," he began.

"You just start the car."

Her tone made him sick but he did so. Once, during the war, he had felt this kind of sick. They had been arguing and after awhile it was like he was empty in the throat, yet then she hadn't foamed at the mouth like this. His big fingers trembled on the wheel.

He stuck the gear-shift in reverse and backed in order to turn around. The earth was soft here. He put it in low, raised the engine and began easing the clutch out.

There was a sharp twanging.

Paal sighed and went to lift the hood. It weighed a ton. He knew exactly what had happened, that it couldn't have been worse; most he could do was bury his face in the engine compartment.

Ida joined him. She too could see the split fibers.

"It broke again, hah?" she said.

Her relenting manner encouraged him to explain. "Ya they didn't have nothing but a used one at that garage and seems it was pretty old."

"I'm leaving," she continued. "From this moment you're on your own and no concern of mine."

Ida gripped her coat collar and marched into the wind. Panicked, he ran after her. She mustn't leave! But he had only the nerve to shout, "You go in that red farmhouse by the highway! That's the landlord! I'll pick you up later!"

That's where he had been drinking and settling the deal; that's why he hadn't come at suppertime. There never was any trouble with the fanbelt.

V. Two Lives

1.

A man was driving towards Fargo. His old Buick didn't like the weather so he was taking it easy on the gas. Let everyone else speed by, he'd get there soon enough. Save gas and you save money and time, he thought; maybe you save yourself too. Just ahead, there was a person walking along the road, a woman in fact. He pulled over, cranked down the window and yelled, "Need a lift someplace!" If she heard him she certainly didn't act it, and it wasn't blowing *that* hard — didn't *see* him either. He shrugged and drove on, peeking once or twice in the rear-view. Anybody that mad looking'll be all right, he said to himself.

South Fargo borders the country at Thirteenth Avenue. Outside of this line, but for an auto court and a filling station and a nursery, there are few marks of civilization. Within it there is shelter.

She crossed the city limit in a trance of rage, unaware of the wind's diminishing. But her feet knew the town and soon she was clumping up Tenth Street. The Fromm house with its grand exterior loomed in the corner of her eye. There she had worked as a maid and nanny and been full of pathetic young dreams. She wasn't about to recall those days, not now.

The breaths whiffled through her teeth as her mind kept ranting, sometimes aloud: For five years he's been taking me in, the whining devil! Well I may be stupid but I know when I'm hoodwinked. That sonofabitch has gone too far, and I'm gonna show him a thing or two. I'm going to rent a room and Peter and I are gonna live there by ourselves, happy as can be, and I'll find a job, *any* job, just so we get by and never see him again. If he sticks his smirking face in the door I'll kill him, *kill* him, and that's all there is to it!

Once she left the underpass behind, the street became North Tenth. She was nearing her destination.

It had been described as "no palace." The rickety outside stairs she had heard about led to an entrance on the third floor. Though her hand was cold, Ida knocked like a policeman; Bee had the radio on full blast.

"*Life Can Be Beautiful,*" an inspiring message of faith drawn from life, brought to you by Spic and Span. . .By the way, how long has it been since you've been to church, where you'll find new assurances that life can be beautiful?

Bee Brandbu was the younger and prettier of the Iverson girls. Her eyes were large and dark blue, and when she hadn't been using pincurls she resembled Joan Fontaine — or so people said. She would have been the same height as Ida only she was born clubfooted; perhaps she would have been as self-effacing too if the teasing of the Hedmark kids had not given her a tongue. Bee's wit and ridicule were something to be feared. When she married her exact opposite, the scowling but gentle Lester Brandbu, people thought it was because she wanted someone she could boss around. Why else pick a simple farmboy? She had followed him to Alabama and California during his stint in the army, and after he was out he had followed her and the tribe. Lester worked hard and let Bee do the thinking. Bee did more than that; she was rarely still. The pincurls were in today.

"*Nei* if it isn't Eeda!" she said, mocking a Norwegian accent.

She could tell that Ida was up in arms and she had a family right to ignore it. Making fun of trouble, no matter what it happened to be, was in the Iverson style.

"Welcome to No Palace. I'll turn this junk off."

The sisters had a lot in common. Both were addicted to soap opera. The place, a converted attic, didn't have much headroom by the walls yet it wasn't tiny; Bee had exaggerated. On tour in her coat and scarf, Ida saw a bed, a kitchen table and a stuffed chair, she saw windows that had no curtains and a hotplate with a knob missing, she saw and she didn't see. Her air was one of disinterest, as though she'd have to be leaving any minute.

"Well, take off your things and have a cup of coffee," said Bee, "or are you just going to stand there like a bill collector?"

Ida knew that she was being observed, that it was time to make an effort.

"I've decided to get a divorce," she said.

Lester was out shopping for a battery so they'd have at least an hour to themselves, and there was no shortage of coffee. Sinking into the stuffed chair, Ida told of her long march. She'd never been able to afford the right kind of shoes anyway, and now this — a ten-mile ordeal! Bee poured hot water in a dishpan and set it at Ida's feet with a look of awe.

Rage carried her along through the whole story. It wasn't until the end, when she thought of little Peter and the dismal weeks to come, that tears interrupted her.

Bee had been listening sympathetically, though she didn't hate the accused. She'd known Paal before Ida met him. He was a nice, lazy Hedmark character who had somehow slipped into the family, a man she didn't have to respect in order to tolerate, and quite harmless; so she was surprised to feel her own anger rising as Ida's broke.

"What are you planning to do then?" she said too loudly. "I'll tell you what *I* plan to do, I'm going straight out there and have a session with him!"

As she stood up she remembered that Lester still had the car. She grabbed the coffee pot and gave them an unneeded third dose.

Ida was sniffling and soaking her feet and seemed better.

"Oh we'll survive, we've got to," she said. "I can always work as a maid and send Peter to the babysitter until I get recertified, then hope there'll be a school job in the middle of the year."

"You be sure and make him pay." Bee didn't like her sister's tone of resignation. "If he won't work and support you, take him in front of the judge. Teach him his duty! There's no other way to handle that kind of guy."

"I spose."

"Suppose nothing! All he did in Seattle was lie on the couch playing hooky when he should have been at the yards, and you let him. We kids didn't want to interfere but we sure saw what was happening. Now maybe *your* eyes have been opened. Have you called Mama?"

The thought of the one person who held this trying life together had a certain effect on both of them. Mama had endured by attending to the practical and not worrying. Things had not been easy for her and she could get mad all right, but when she acted it was to help the family. Anger is a waste, busy your hands instead: this she had endlessly demonstrated to her children.

Soon Ida was drying her feet and Bee was taking care of the dishes. It seemed best that Ida stay overnight, though she'd have only the floor to sleep on. The man downstairs had told Bee and Lester that they could use his phone if they didn't wear it out, so Ida would call the estate and let Mama know of the change in plans. Bee would drive her there in the morning to get Peter and a suitcase or two, then bring her into town again; that was as far ahead as either of them cared to think.

The man wasn't at home weekdays but left his door unlocked, and Ida thanked God she could make the call in private. It was bad enough knowing that every rubberneck around would be on the line. That's how it was in the country. She heard a distant dull ringing, one long and three short, and imagined Papa getting up from his solitaire.

"*Hellaw!* Iverson talkin!"

"Hello Papa, it's me. Could I speak to Mama?"

"Hah?!"

"It's Ida. I'd like to talk to Mama."

"Eeda is it? Ya, hang on."

As she waited she strained to catch the small sounds of home, but with God knows how many farmwives listening in she couldn't hear much. Mama didn't even greet her; she was all upset about the snow and hoped they wouldn't be so foolish as to travel.

Was it snowing? She would have noticed coming down the steps, or Bee, who had gone to the corner store, would have seen it. Ida peered out the man's window. Against the dark background of the neighboring house, flurries were visible. Wake up girl, she thought.

"It must have just started here, but that's fine. I'm staying over with Bee anyhow. We'll be back tomorrow unless they close the roads."

"Well there *is* a storm warning." said Mama to underline her point.

Then she brought Peter to the phone. His solemn innocent voice made Ida tremble. She felt as if she were a runaway, or calling from jail, and might never see him again.

Bee was toiling up the stairs. That must be an awful climb for her!

She didn't want Peter to know she was crying. There were rubbernecks too. "You say bye-bye to Gramma and Grandpa for me, and be a good boy till we get home!" She put some change on the man's table and readied herself for a slap of wind, a slap she deserved.

The storm seemed to fall rather than sweep through between the buildings. The snow was fine as sand, and as gritty.

Bee sat smoking a cigarette, her wide eyes quick with anger. "This is too early for a blizzard. We should have stayed in Seattle. Where's that husband of mine? Uff-da!"

It was neither the storm nor Lester's absence that had renewed Bee's rage, of this Ida was sure. But at any rate she had to have a tissue, so she went to the bathroom and got one.

"You almost had a visitor," said Bee.

"Oh?"

"Ya I saw him park in front when I was leaving the store and that's all the farther he got."

"Oh."

Ida's trembles disappeared. So he'd had the gall to follow her after what happened, the absolute gall, and after pretending he didn't have the address! That man was a standing, walking lie.

"I simply asked what Mr. Malmlund had to say for himself and he made a sheep-dog face and wanted to talk to you — of course! — but I said it was a nice day for a ride to Hickson so why didn't he go buy another fanbelt, if you chose to talk to him that was your business, but he's not welcome in my house as far as I'm concerned."

The tip of Bee's cigarette fumed and crackled.

"I'll have one of those too if you don't mind," said Ida, who never smoked. "You did the right thing."

They glared at each other, then laughed.

Now that Ida had resolved that *she* was doing the right thing also, they could settle into a normal afternoon visit. Bee talked about herself and Lester and the little they had accomplished. They had intended to get work immediately, but it was more fun chasing around the country hunting pheasants and drinking beer; the weather had been irresistible. They would have to get on the stick sooner or later, the savings wouldn't last, yet Bee didn't seem particularly concerned. Ida said that she had never looked so happy.

Bee laughed again. "It must be the North Dakota air."

They discussed the state of the family, Jim's expected return, how

Aunt Martha and Uncle Aaron were faring in Seattle, if Oliver and Edith were on the road yet, poor Lyle and the booze and so forth, and they agreed with Mama; home was the place to be. You could survive anywhere but you couldn't *live* away from the old haunts. Ya Mama had known — and Papa, he was the same as usual.

"Those big politicians still come to see him," said Ida. "Maybe business is improving, and wouldn't that be wonderful."

The sisters touched on every item of interest but one: Paal. At such a moment he was easily and well forgotten.

Lester arrived with a box in his arm and a crabby mouth. Believing the weatherman's promises, he'd worn only a light summer jacket. The storm had caught him. He was getting sore throat and had bought a pint of rum just in case. Lester was a strapping young fellow who hadn't missed a day's work in his life. He nodded to Ida.

"You found a battery though," said Bee. Her account of Ida's predicament was brief. There had been a quarrel and Ida was going to spend the night. No sense troubling Lester.

He grunted and went to fiddle with the radio. The weatherman didn't deserve a second chance but Lester had to know how long they'd be trapped inside. He was drinking from the bottle.

The Iversons had been willing to overlook his mental shortcomings because he seemed to be a plain, ordinary good husband, and Ida had been the first to accept him. Yet now he had changed the mood of the room. She felt like a guest, that more sisterly talk would be impolite.

Bee turned the conversation to Seattle, a vivid, distracting subject, and Ida got her smile back. The thought of Seattle had never been so lovely. She defended it with vigor against Bee's criticisms. Meanwhile the storm tore at the roof and the radio kept chattering.

"Can't hear for shit," said Lester, "but sounds like it's gonna quit by evening."

Bee glanced at the window. "Say that reminds me. We were thinking of seeing 'The Lost Weekend' tonight. If it's snowing too bad we can walk, I spose. How about it, Eeda? Since you're here you might as vell go *vitt!*"

But Ida lowered her head and didn't answer at once. Movies were for those who had earned some entertainment, regular men and women, not her. She was alone.

"If it's snowing too bad we can walk, I spose," Lester added.

"Oh I'd rather stay and listen to the radio."

They ate as soon as it was dark; Bee and Lester wanted to get to the showing at ten to seven. They hadn't argued with Ida, she needed time to herself, but Bee did ask the loan of her wool coat. She told Lester that she could use a snort of that rum too, enough to make it to the Roxy, and she finished the bottle as they left. Ida would be doing the dishes.

She stood in the doorway watching her poor brave sister limp into the night. The wind raved on but it was clearing. That meant cold tomorrow. She had to hand it to Bee who had done so well and never let that handicap get in her way. She had found a man she could lean on too.

Confronted with a strange empty apartment, Ida knew that she should have gone along; the isolation would be terrible. She wasn't cut out for this. She wasn't cut out for marriage either. What *was* she cut out for? When oh when in Jesus' name would she come to port?

2

The speck that was Ida did not stop at the farmhouse. He hadn't been hoping, just watching. A dog, some flea-bitten red stray, had approached and sat watching him in turn. Paal took a hunk of sandwich from the ground and dusted it off to eat. Picking up another, he threw it towards the dog.

"Here skipper, there's a lot more!" His voice sounded feeble but the dog understood it.

If he didn't replace that belt now he'd have to do it later; he'd better move. He opened the rumble seat and got his tool chest and extra fanbelt, the one he always carried, and began the job. It was hard to loosen those fittings. He sweated in spite of the weather. When he was done he had a reeking shirt and grease on his face and jacket.

He would have liked a swig of coffee, both for his throat and to rinse the dirt out; what he hadn't swallowed with the bread remained in his teeth. But there was nothing to drink, nothing for him at all.

Thinking he should keep a tool handy, he tucked his good wrench under the seat. That's where he saw the envelope. It must have fallen down. He stared at Bee's handwriting until he had memorized the address.

"Bye boy!" he said to the cautious lurking dog. "I gotta go fetch my wife!"

Paal hadn't been touching his snoose, but as the engine warmed he indulged in a big pinch. He also dug out a handkerchief and tried to remove the worst of the smudges. In order to check his face he had to wipe off the mirror. There's a sick-looking bastard, he thought.

The dog's eyes followed a 1934 Pontiac as it went hobbling over the ruts.

It would have been nice to catch up with her, simply to have a talk with nobody listening, but Ida must have set quite a pace. When he came to Tenth Street, the wind he was bucking turned from gray to white and he drove scared. He could hardly tell if there was anyone on the sidewalks, the snow was so thick. He pictured her lost and frozen in the storm.

How much time had he spent on that damn belt, an hour? She couldn't have done five miles in that. Well she might have got a ride or called Bee for one.

Panic made it easier to find the address, but as soon as he ran into his sister-in-law he knew that the emergency was over. Bee's expression was enough to indicate that the Iversons had declared war on Paul

Malmlund; what she said didn't bother him. At least Ida was safe.

Bee just clutched her grocery bag and let him have it. Paal just stood. Somewhere in that tall unfriendly house was Ida. At least she was safe and would know he'd been here.

In wild weather, most Fargoans hurry home. Even the stores are deserted. The city becomes impassive. Those who can't or won't go home may gather at a place like the Amidon Bar to wait it out.

There was no one on the streets to observe the black Pontiac as it headed slowly downtown, but outside the Amidon there were plenty of cars. He had five dollars and thirteen cents to rinse his teeth with and put gas in the buggy; meanwhile he could do some figuring.

He heard the men complaining even before he got in. Yesterday's crowd had grown. The regulars, only more of them, were three deep at the bar. He managed to plant an elbow on it and order a tap.

The barkeep recognized Paal. "That brother of yours isn't coming, is he? We had to bounce him. Lucky we didn't sic the police on him."

The drinkers paid no attention. They already had something to talk about, and a main grievance: the weather. They were laughing.

"I don't know," said Paal, "but he's no brother of mine I can assure you."

"Well, we don't want him."

It occurred to Paal that he would have to do his thinking fast. Ida would be sleeping at Bee's tonight, they wouldn't travel in the storm, and that was good. They'd probably go out to Iversons' tomorrow. But where in hell was *he* supposed to sleep?

He guessed they had called the farm and set the old folks against him. He'd get no comfort there. The roads might be blocked anyway. He considered the shanty, it had a stove, but in cold like this he'd need more than wood; too late to shop for a sack of briquettes; he didn't have much money either.

Paal spent fifteen cents on a second large glass. Soon he'd be down to four and a half and it was six o'clock. The barkeep turned up the radio in honor of the news.

We have learned the bitter lesson that the weakness of this great republic invites men of ill will to shake the very foundations of civilization all over the world.

Two bucks would cover the gas, leaving say another two-fifty to spend. Oh a dollar's worth in the tank would give him a roundtrip to Iversons', then he'd have three and a half. He could always flop at the mission or someplace cheap like that. On say three dollars and fifty cents he'd neither thirst nor freeze, and he mustn't forget to have a sandwich. Paal's hunger had been slumbering, but as the long day's chill wore off it stirred in him.

If the news of the world had failed to interest the men, they did take notice of the weather news. Snow ending, clear and cold tomorrow, the radio said; an overnight low of ten degrees.

That settled, he bought a bag of nuts. Another bag and another tap made the stool feel pretty good. He had done his share of running around, by God, smiling and yakking to strangers, and all to please a fussy woman. They should have been at the farm now, he and Ida, with their chairs next to the stove and a pot of coffee and the kid, that's where they belonged, but she had to go and have a mood and put everything out of whack. If she was so worried about money, why did she strand him in a bar? Well he'd just sit here then.

In time, the evening and the place and the beer flowed together to a point of clarity. At last he understood the nature of life, could almost *see* it.

Paal didn't remember what the man at his elbow had been saying, but the glow in his mind seemed to contradict it. He turned to enlighten him. "No you got it wrong. You gotta look at the whole. That Karl Marx fellow never owned anything so you won't find a house in dialect materialism, and a house is what I mean. Otherwise you can't live. It's all a matter of walls and a roof and human privacy, and I don't mean boozhwah. Life is a house, *forstaar du*. Get yourself a nice simple shanty out on the range, may not be spotless but who goddamn cares? You wanna live, don't goddamn listen to the womenfolks!"

They were laughing and slapping his shoulder, and the radio was singing kiss me once and kiss me twice and kiss me once again, but that didn't spoil it. Finally he had said what he had seen; he deserved congratulations. He could laugh too, by God.

"I think Billy Conn's the real contender," Marx told someone else.

"'Livet er et hus', sa'n!'"

"Ya well it is!" said Paal.

"He doesn't belong in there with the heavyweights."

Walls and a roof, that's all you have to have, and never mind the stink. The leaves may grow and fall, but you got things to do. Dead animals are a part of it. He understood so well that even Ida'd see and be willing to talk it over.

Happiness carried him to the pay phone.

Once she heard him out that'd be it. But the operator couldn't find any Brandbu listed. Repeating the name didn't help.

"When you get ahold of her say that I'm gonna roll up in that there blanket and sleep in the car and the next time she sees me I'll be stiff as a board!"

"Keep an eye on that guy," said Marx.

The phone gave him his money back; one nickle, Nikolina.

His eyes were damp. Sure's hot in this joint, he figured.

VI. Common Sense

Every morning but Sunday, after oatmeal and tea, he would go to Hedmark, a two-mile drive with a post office box at the end. He could have had the mail brought by rural carrier only it was too much trouble, and in law practice an unchanging town address was the thing to have. Besides, he had to fetch water, the landlady hadn't revived the well, and there was shopping to be done and visiting with the old timers, so every morning but Sunday he'd take a five-gallon can and a grocery bag, crank up the Model-A and hit the road. He received a lot of mail, most of it in the forenoon dispatch which came out of Fargo. Later the same truck would deliver mail from Wahpeton and the south, but the afternoon dispatch was meager, nothing in it that couldn't wait, and it was only on Saturday that his humpbacked figure could be seen working the town pump at four o'clock.

In his weather diary he had recorded a noon high of sixty and a low of eighteen at bedtime; the temperature had dropped forty-two degrees in the storm. When he got up he could feel the chill and knew that the Model-A wouldn't start, but he prepared to go to Hedmark anyway, even tried the crank as Jensine looked on from the window. The engine would turn over easy by afternoon. Ole Hrolf Iverson would be making but one public appearance this Saturday.

28 October, he wrote. *Temp. 11 above 8:45 a.m. Clear and no wind. About one inch dry snow, some drifts. Squirrel tracks near the tub.*

The first snow of the year awakened his first memory: white hill, red sled. He had to have been three or less, for they had left Norway in the summer of 1881, joining his father at the Dakota homestead, and there were no hills here. What he remembered was not simply a place or an object but an inclusive joy, the red sled had been his and life good, so if the neighbors sulked in the coming of winter O.H. Iverson took heart. The first snow made him think of better times.

He went back into the house to return the can and the grocery bag, also to get his rifle. He smiled at Peter who was sitting in Jensine's lap. "The car says he doesn't vant to start," he said. "Now vhat ve gonna do, *brodern?*"

Peter hurried to check under the lid of the water can. "There's nothing in it!"

"Nothing, not a drop! I guess ve have to melt snow to drink."

Peter watched him as he wrested the .22 out of a bunch of standing mop handles in the closet and pocketed some shells. Grandpa had kept his big black coat on and that meant something.

"Ya *brodern,* all ve can do now is take a valk."

"I want to go too, said Peter.

There was a movement of alarm in Jensine's corner. "Oh it's much too cold for a walk, and you don't have a good jacket. You can be out with me after while."

O.H. Iverson stepped to the door. "I spose they von't get here till noon, Eeda and her husband," he said in a voice that was not a grandfather's.

But Jensine was talking to the child again.

He headed west out of the farmstead grove. The earth wasn't hard frozen yet and the snow lay in uncertain gray streaks over the black plowing. This sun will melt it, he thought. His two o'clock drive would be easy.

Ahead, right in the middle of the section, rose the old Johannesson woods. Hans Johannesson had arrived in 1880, just like O.H.'s father, had staked his claim along what used to be the Wahpeton-Fargo road, built a shack, planted trees and seeded his wife, and there was nothing unusual in any of that, but the government surveyors had news for him. It must have been around the time of statehood, 1889, that they finished work on the county and Hans learned that his farm was in the wrong place. The road was to be eliminated. Oh he could keep a driveway but it would be a half mile long and he'd have to maintain it himself. Hans Johannesson didn't enjoy living in the middle of the section, still he hung on for some years. Was it 1896 or '97 that he pulled out and bought a farm on the Minnesota side? Now, other than a few scraps of lumber and a rusted riding plow, only the woods itself remained as testimony. No one went there, it was too far in, so Hans's Eden had become a small game refuge. O.H. Iverson was walking in that direction, his rifle handy.

The air didn't smell but the snow gave it an edge. He moved in silence through the massive silence of the field, glad to be way from the house. Other men his age, and he could name them, were broken in body and whimpering of death. They had wasted their lives in mindless action, drunk when they should have been reading, eaten whatever their women dished up, and if they were bedridden in age it was all their own fault. He had taken care of *his* health; unlike them, he'd used his brains. The wages of ignorance, to be trapped in the hot and busy rooms where womenfolks dominated, were not for O.H. Iverson.

As a kid he had looked after horses. The body is a horse and the mind does the looking after. Treat it well and it stays fit. Drink tea, not coffee; wine, one glass at night, nothing stronger. Eat fish, blood sausage and salt pork, not that raw stuff; potatoes and cabbage and rice and oatmeal, never the junk they seal in tin. Plenty of water and exercise and a couple of bran muffins a day will flush the guts. The horse's needs are simple.

He was footing as light as a colt, so he mustn't have been too wrong. But a horse is not important. Look after it well and it doesn't have to be thought about; then the mind can attend to important things.

The stupid ruined themselves getting drunk and sick and chasing around the country, with them the mind is the horse, and his sons and daughters were no exception. He had showed them how to live but instead they followed Jensine's way of ignorance. Ida and Bee he could pardon as mere womenfolks, but look at Oliver, and Jim, and Lyle. They could work hard and take orders and that was it, not an ounce of brains among them. If they did try to think, it was about money or where they should run to next, and all that they got from Jensine. Well he had done his part, brought them into the world and set a good example; the boys were on their own, so was he.

Far to the south were the unmistakable slim cottonwoods of the Iverson homeplace. He had grown up there. Then he had been on his own too, different from his quite ordinary siblings in that he wanted to leave and seek an education. He was the eldest son, the heir, and Hrolf said no and would have kept him on the farm had he not been, at twenty, the bigger man. One day O.H. had carried a giant rock out of the field, Hrolf couldn't have budged it, and that ended the arguing. His father only asked that he promise to return if called. He went on to normal school and the university, was home summers to help, entered the legal profession, married, and opened an office in the west, and when he heard the call he came. But it was too late.

He stopped to see if he could make out the buildings. His sister Ingeborg would be sitting in the house, afraid to leave it unguarded. Dishonest people fear dishonesty in others. It was she who had robbed him of the place, who had moved in with her kid husband to supervise the old man's death. Father's note had been urgent, shakily written, so he had closed the Williston office, put Jensine, Ida, Oliver and everything they owned in the car and rushed home. There lay Hrolf, barely able to speak, pretending not to have sent the letter, and there sat Ingeborg, the deed already in her pocket.

The white-painted house used to shine out of the grove. Now it was indistinguishable from the barn. He had not been there or talked to her since.

"Ya you just vait in your cell," said O.H. Iverson.

Some thought that when he left the valley Hrolf had given up on him, some that Hrolf was not right in the head at the last so the transfer of the deed was illegal. A sharp attorney like him could contest it. But O.H. didn't listen to prattle. Moreover he wasn't one for suing relatives; he was above that.

Trouble with this country, it was too easy to be dishonest. Take Bill Langer and Bill Lemke. He had read law with the both of them at the University of North Dakota, knew them well and could say that they were intelligent men but dealers. Especially Langer, he was willing to do almost anything to come out on top. Lemke's dealings were more covert; in his days as kingmaker of the Non-Partisan League he had learned to work through friends. O.H. supposed they acted as they had to, and they had always treated him with respect. (There were many Norwegians going to the polls, something those Germans didn't forget.) Bill Lemke, erstwile champion of the underdog, had done him a good turn in 1934. What was it the letter said?

I recommended you to Judge Miller for appointment as Conciliation Commissioner for Richland County. The Bankruptcy Law provides that the Conciliation Commissioner shall act as lawyer for the farmer. It is my desire that this law be administered with fairness and justice to all.

It was hard times for the little guy. O.H. had taught those mortgage-holders a lesson to remember. Lemke got his support. But O.H. was also one of the Republicans backing Roosevelt, whom Lemke hated, so when he ran for County Judge the NPL shunned him. He lost. No doubt the sonsaguns had expected him to drop FDR out of thankfulness and curry favor with *them* — and an appointment to the Conciliation Commission led nowhere.

Some men would have played by their rules, not he. Langer and Lemke had a political game and to hell with the issues. One was in the Senate and the other in the House, and it was hard times as usual for O.H. Iverson.

The abandoned woods stood high in front of him. Seeing rabbit tracks in the swatches of snow, he paused to load the gun.

Most people don't know right from wrong. The few that do should be in government. Government should be a matter of honest dealing. How else will the people learn and in a country like this who else will instruct them? But what happens in this country, the stupid elect the ignorant so a man has to play ignorant in order to get in and only the shrewd, not the honest, dealers can succeed. As a result, people are at the mercy of the government that should be helping them.

Roosevelt was a *jarl* out of the ancient sagas, a wise autocrat, a slick operator but a right-minded one. He understood the American people, that they needed rule from above, not the freedom to make mistakes. He sought to enlarge the powers of government so that the average citizen would be protected from the dealings of the shrewd and taught a better life. That's why the mainstreet Republicans were after him, hollering *too much government* and that he was limiting the freedom of the individual. Those connivers didn't care about the average idiot. All they wanted was for government to serve big business.

People were like this Hans Johannesson, an uneducated Swede and dumb to begin with, they always got in trouble or created it when there was no one there telling them what to do. O.H. snickered as he recalled Hans's moving day, the sight of the full wagons shambling down to the Mora bridge. That had meant one less Swede west of the Red, one less uninformed vote in North Dakota. The Swedes knew nothing of self-government, having been for centuries under the kings' thumb, cannon-fodder and proud of it, and moving to America hadn't changed their slavishness. Here they bent the knee to petty politicians. Oh the Swedes had a poet or two, Esais Tegnér was all right, but even though O.H. could read the original, he preferred *"Frithiofs Saga"* in the Danish version:

> Som Fosterbørn i Hildings Bo
> der voxed unge Planter to;
> ej før saa Norden to saa skjønne;
> de voxed herligt i det Grønne.

He should be quiet now, might scare the game. Unmittening his trigger hand, he began a slow circuit of the woods. There were more than two *Planter i Johannessons Bo* but every one leafless and still. Some little gray and white birds were creeping on the trunks, otherwise no activity. It had been green *i det Grønne* when Hans — ya it was in the summer, the summer of 1897, that Hans left.

O.H. Iverson had kept his memory in shape. Memory was partner to thought. The old god of gods had had a raven sitting on each shoulder, Hugin and Munin, Thought and Memory, and listening to them he got to be wise. That was Odin. That was the Norwegian heritage.

Those fool Swedes had Tegnér but no one to put up against Henrik Ibsen, no one the match of Bjørnson or Wergeland either. Why? Because the Swedes were not only allergic to freedom, they couldn't stand to *think*. A man who won't think soon deteriorates in body as well as mind, nor is he capable of *action*. The Swedes who stayed home were no better than the ones that came over here. When Hitler invaded Norway they just closed their eyes and went on selling to him; and brave Norwegians were dying in the hills and towns for love of independence. The Norwegians understood, as Cousin Marie had written, that it was either fight or give up your right to exist. The Swedes had already lost the ability to understand. They couldn't think. They wanted their masters to do the thinking for them.

A solitary brown leaf dangled near the end of an upper limb. There was a shot. The leaf fell intact: he had split its twig at thirty yards.

Well he couldn't blame Hans Johannesson and the average American voter for being what they were. People are ignorant, willing and needing to be led. But, in a country like this, too often they get bad masters.

He had finished his round. Splayed boot prints trailed in from the east. It was time to put on the mitten and go home, say to hell with the rabbits, but he wished the trek were longer. He was in no hurry to be inside again.

He who is to lead must take the path from ignorance to knowledge, and it's more than half a mile to the end. If he's a poor Norwegian-speaking farm kid, the going will be rough. He'll have to set his shoulder to the *wheel*. But once he gets there he will be an educated man.

It was O.H.'s education that had raised him above others. As he walked east he looked down on the flat country.

Ya who'd have thought that the silly little boy with his red sled would someday be reading Cicero and Mommsen and presenting cases in an American court of law? That he should also learn to appreciate the music of Pietro Mascagni and Ole Bull had been unforeseen, no one had planned it; nor had anyone said that he should be a columnist for *Normanden,* that paper in Grand Forks. Some had rich family behind them, not O.H. He had found the path himself and reached the end of it all alone.

A love of knowledge was a love of independence, the Norwegian example proved it, and he wasn't ashamed to be of that stock. Surely no Yankee or Englishman could have done what he had. The English were an untrustworthy race and the Yankees a mixed one; the language they shared seemed inferior. Oh he didn't hold with the Quisling racial nonsense. He remembered the simple Norwegian farmer who had come to his office and said, "I need a monkey." O.H. had almost thrown him out. But if one fool couldn't tell the difference between *advokat* and *apekatt* it wasn't the fault of the Norwegian language. Every race had a majority of idiots. His native tongue was a compact, precise instrument, like Ole Bull's violin. (Yet imagine the Hedmark town fiddler getting his hands on it!)

"So buy a mirror!" he had told him. But he accepted the case. That was long ago in the hopeful Williston time.

As a young lawyer he had been thinking of the governorship. He had begun to establish a name in Williston, where the Norwegian vote counted, and might have run for state's attorney had Hrolf not called him home. Many wanted him to return to the west, Lemke did, the NPL was growing out there, but O.H. knew he'd be wise to stay in Hedmark. He would achieve the governorship only by way of local politics, and there were more people in the east. He also intended to keep an eye on Ingeborg. The law may not have respected his right of primogeniture, but he could afford to wait. So he had rented a desk in a corner of the bank lobby and hung a shingle outside.

Business, in the '20s, was nothing to complain of; farmers were starting to get rich and the town too. But people seemed to expect a lawyer to be as crooked as they — as if they deserved not to pay any taxes! O.H. had always turned them down and given them a short course in legality to boot. When he became state's attorney he'd show them! He had campaigned everywhere, even in Barney and Fairmount, talked and spent money like a fool, yet it was all for naught. His reputation for honesty had ruined him. No votes, and a dwindling business. Oh he wasn't going to give up, not O.H. Iverson, and if it hadn't been for the Crash his hopes might well have survived. But history took over.

The forces of history and of nature run the world. Mankind lives in their grip. When there come drought and depression it's *hard times* and people can't do a thing about it.

He was approaching the farmstead. Only the yellow of two big trees, an ash and a cottonwood, relieved the gray. Smoke angled up from the gray house. Now back in to Jensine, he thought. Perhaps Ida would be here, then he'd have more than *brodern* and his pipe to look forward to.

In hard times the ignorant were too ready to jump on each other and blame the next guy, just as Jensine had so often blamed him for the situation he hadn't caused and was helpless to change. It wasn't his fault that nobody stopped at the bank anymore. Pockets were empty. Thousands of dollars were owing him, but how does one collect what isn't there? After the banks closed he moved his books home and sat instead at a table in the rear of the cafe. People knew where they could find him; thus he remained in business. Once in a while he brought a client to the house, though he preferred not to: with kids underfoot and Jensine hollering it was no place for gentlemen. He also spent the evenings uptown. Some farmers and merchants used to play whist at the bar till midnight, and he'd join in an occasional game. A lawyer had to make himself available, didn't he? Jensine had no right to criticize. What did she need him at home for anyway? The kids got along fine by themselves. As to the rest, it wasn't O.H. who had split the marriage bed in 1922! "Nothing in the house to eat," she said? How about the free food her mother was always sending in, eggs, potatoes, cabbage, rhubarb?

She should have been looking after the kids, teaching them good manners, but no, she had to bitch. When she didn't have anything to blame him for, she'd invent some trifle. Women are the lowest of the ignorant. We should never have allowed them to vote.

Seeing that Paal Malmlund's car was not in the yard, he stayed in the grove a few minutes. He could shoot rabbits here as well as at Johannesson's. But the snow was decaying, the spoor with it; and little Peter might be outside.

Ya it was *hard times* but he had come through, more than he could say for a lot of people. It had kicked the stuffing out of the bigshots and driven the trash to the cities. Holding his own in Hedmark had been no mean accomplishment. Yet, in fact, business seemed to improve. Those who'd gone to somebody else in the '20s were now happy to talk to O.H. Iverson. No doubt they figured on getting a cheap attorney. He refused several, and it was a hell of a chore collecting from those he had dared to take on.

Ya what would have happened to Jensine's parents had not the Conciliation Commissioner stepped in? They would have lost the farm! Then there was the case of Ingeborg and her husband. It still tickled him to remember the tears of that overgrown brat — she'd lacked the courage to approach O.H. herself — as he whined about the threat of foreclosure. And O.H. had saved Jensine's parents and Ingeborg too and it didn't cost any of them one red cent!

The try for county judge, with the NPLers pretending he didn't exist, was not quite so disappointing as the earlier race had been. His opponent had won by a mere two hundred. It seemed that in *hard times* the fools were willing to *think*. While on the stump he had attacked religion, all kinds: not only the religion of Jesus Christ or Karl Marx but that of Henry Ford as well. He let them know that the improvement of man's estate was not to be found in dreams of a better tomorrow but in exercising common sense today. To his surprise they had been ready to listen, even to argue. Oh he was no candidate to please the churchmen or the amateur socialists or those who worshipped the dollar, but he thought he had what it took to swing the election. If his opponent hadn't gone courting the womenfolks, speaking at ladies' aids and so on, O.H. would have won it.

He heard a clattering. Jensine was out with a stick to break up the ice in her rain pails. In her bulky gray coat and pointed hat she looked like a clean-shaven dwarf. Peter stood watching her and O.H. watched from the trees. They hadn't noticed him.

The church basements had defeated him — women's superstition and piety. Ingeborg had stolen his land. Ingeborg and Jensine and their whole ingorant breed had kept him off the bench. Poor little Peter, if he just knew what kind of a world this is!

He'd try again. The war had set things back, returning the shrewd and the moneymad to power, and at first he had opposed getting into it. He had agreed with the aviator, old Lindbergh's boy. There was a Swede who had something between the ears! But Pearl Harbor left Roosevelt no choice, or him. The Japs and the Germans had to be destroyed. Well the insanity was over and now people were in for it. No more jobs, no more defense contracts, no more government regulation. The next Crash was already happening. That Missouri farm hick couldn't stop it; he was too small a man. *It was coming hard times.* O.H. would try again.

He went to the rear of the house so that Jensine wouldn't spot him, then sneaked to the door and entered chuckling.

The forenoon vanished in the pages of Gjerset's history of Norway. O.H. became insensible to the room, no longer heard the squeak of his wood rocker or the voices of Jensine and the child; his mind was on King Harald Hardradi's death and the year was 1066. Not until other sounds encroached did he remove the cold pipe from his lips in North Dakota. The clock was marking the hour of one.

"G'dagen," said Lester Brandbu.

A different car was sitting where Paal Malmlund's should have been and Bee, not Paal, was with Ida and Jensine in the kitchen. O.H. surveyed the son-in-law who had turned up.

"Vell vhat do you know?"

"Not much, I guess."

That's true, thought O.H. Iverson. At least he wouldn't have to entertain a fellow like this, who had a bottle of beer to keep him happy.

He looked in at the kitchen door, but the womenfolks were in a huddle and too busy jabbering to greet him.

Lester had slumped into a chair. "Pretty bad weather we had."

"Bullshit," said O.H., grinning. "There's no such thing as bad veather.

If it shines, it shines; if it storms, it storms. Vhat occurs is veather and is neither good nor bad!"

"Oh ya."

That was enough wasted on this fellow. O.H. sat down again. He wanted to finish the Chicago Sunday papers, they arrived in the mail each week, and he felt tired.

Lester Brandbu didn't mind the neglect. As his father-in-law read, he went out to the Dodge to get more beer and returned in amiable silence.

But after ten minutes O.H. Iverson spoke: "Have you seen Paal then?"

"No I think he and Ida had a fight."

"Hah?"

"No I say I think they had a fight. We just brought her out to get the kid and some stuff, that's all I know."

"Oh."

The newspaper soon lay folded on the rug. O.H. still wasn't paying attention to his guest; he seemed to be listening. The rocker didn't move.

"Anyone — " it was Ida " — who could bring me to a place like that, treat me like that, must have something radically wrong with him, and there's no two ways about it. The filth was simply *indescribable*. You would have to have been there, Mama. I'd think he'd have a *little* consideration for his wife and son, but nossir, not Paal!"

Bee: "It wasn't just the place, Mama. It was the fact he lied. He told her one lie after another. She should have left him years ago, that's what I always said and Oliver too."

Jensine was hard to hear. "But you don't mean to divorce him, do you? It wouldn't be right. A woman can't go and live by herself, and with a child, that's no good. You best talk it over."

"You don't understand, Mama," said Bee, "she's already tried to talk. But Paal doesn't care what she says. In this day and age a woman doesn't have to put up with that kind of treatment."

Ida: "No I made up my mind. He's a losing proposition, and since I'll have nothing to do with him anyway it might as well be divorce."

O.H. Iverson jumped to his feet, leaving the rocker in motion. "Time to go to town," he said. "Lester, you vant to help me start the Model-A?"

"Oh ya."

The men's appearing hushed the kitchen. O.H. went about his preparations slowly, donning scarf, coat, cap and gloves, finding the grocery box and the water can, and ignored his audience. But the women had their eyes to the floor, as though they were praying. Lester sighed as he buttoned his jacket. It was at the last moment that O.H. turned to speak:

"You *knaw,* the human race can't function vithout social institutions. People who don't respect these institutions are no better than savages. *A voman belongs vith her husband and that's that."*

Then he strode chuckling into the milder air of the afternoon and the engine awoke and he was off to meet the public.

VII. Vale's Edge

The Dodge departed while the Model-A was out. Girls are too independent now, Jensine was thinking as she waved; they have so many funny ideas. They leave home and go and do what they please, no one to check up on them, and soon there's trouble. Divorce is not only a sin, it's unheard of. In olden times the girls weren't even supposed to mention it.

"Bye," said Peter, his small hand opening and closing.

What sort of life would it be for the child, no man in the house, and what would people say? Jensine was glad that her mother had not survived to see this.

Peter wanted to get back in. She patted his head as he tried to work the knob.

At least Ida had agreed to stay and talk, she listened *that* much, so maybe it wasn't too late. Better to think things over where a person could relax than to sit with Bee in town.

She was standing in the early twilight of the kitchen, arms limp in front of her. When Peter came and embraced her leg, she too touched him; but she didn't look up at Mama.

Ida felt broken, not of heart but in spirit. Well she had resisted Bee, who'd gone off spitting nails in rage, and kept to her own course. It was just that the deciding had been too effortless — not like a choice, more like a meek acceptance of the sensible.

"Days are really getting short," she said. "Oh I wish it would be nice again."

Mama's answer was to fill a lamp with kerosene as she resumed the doleful monologue that her absence from the room had interrupted:

"Ya and Mildred, Art Johnson's girl, was married and living in Fergus Falls and then she went and got a job in the cafe and pretty soon was running around, and the child wasn't even three but wouldn't you know she just left it alone in the house, said to her husband, 'You look after it — I got other interests!' and he couldn't think what to do, she was so terrible. Then one day she asked for a divorce, but he was from good family — son to a businessman there — and he simply couldn't believe *his own wife* should say such a word. 'Divorce?' Why nobody in her right mind would even *think* it. So 'no' he says and let me tell you she didn't come home that night or the next, she was gone, and her folks never saw her again either who had tried so hard to do well by Mildred."

Mama's mouth wasn't quite in a straight line; however, one hint of contention would put it there. Ida took some wooden matches from the dispenser on the wall and advanced cautiously.

"I remember Mildred," she said. "She was always like that though."

In the flare of the mantle, Mama's lips looked ready for coffee. There'd be that rather than a fight. The lamp made evening of the afternoon. Peter seemed tired; Ida led him away to nap. When she returned, the cups were on the table.

"Where you gonna live then?" Mama sounded sterner than she appeared.

Time to be frank, thought Ida. "I don't know. I don't know anything. I never dreamed it would come to this. Uff-da."

"Ya well he did find some kind of place."

"It's the *deceit,* Mama, the *deceit!*" But Ida's exasperation didn't last; she was worn out. "I realized long ago he wasn't the man I hoped he would be. Paal doesn't have it in him. He *can't* get a job — he doesn't have what it takes. Even if I stayed with him, *I'd* have to go back to work and support the family. Then he could stop his lying and sit home as much as he wants. But when I go back to work again it's gonna be for *something,* not him. He's had plenty chances. So why bother? Mama, if there were any way of avoiding this I'd jump at it, I really would."

Mama put work-rough fingers on her hand. "The world is a vale of tears," she said quietly. "Ya and *I* could tell you a thing or two. You just have to learn to think of the good of others before your own."

It was either speak or cry: "I wish I was Mildred Johnson! She doesn't care! But I don't know what to do!"

"All we can do now is take a walk," said Peter.

He stood on the threshhold, his bright round eyes not sleepy at all.

Ida, who had no excuse to laugh, laughed. Mama took in the scene with an approving snicker.

It was a good idea; she ought to be giving him more attention. As they stepped outside, the enthusiastic Peter leading, Ida sensed warmth in the air. Had it changed on the trip down? She couldn't remember. When you get so upset you don't know what's around you, that's bad, she thought. They wouldn't have needed these extra scarves and sweaters, not now, but Mama would see it differently; better wear them.

The snow had melted everywhere but under a few trees, and the brownish-green yard was turning soggy. Lester's car had churned up some mud. The whole earth was bedraggled. Today they'd have gumbo to avoid. But the sky, if nothing else, was clean and there was a promise of south wind.

Peter ran wildly towards the road. He had been in the house too much and needed exercise. Might as well try the township road, she figured. A little wet snow remained in the ditch there.

They strolled on the high shoulder along the woods of the farmstead grove which merged with that of another, but unoccupied, farmstead to the south. Though Peter was ahead, he didn't go in the car-lane; his Seattle training had been thorough. The trees ended and they were moving in sunlight. She could see, less than a mile off, her grandfolks' place. Uncle Alvin lived and worked there now.

Just to the right of the road, isolated and empty, stood the country school she and the rest of the kids had attended. It was all familiar ground, but being on it didn't help her. She was under a load of sadness.

"Stay with Mama!" she called pointlessly.

Bee's grim headshaking was understandable. "No but you're caving in, Ida. Next thing you'll be back where you started." But Ida felt she deserved more credit than that. The resolution had been made, she was leaving Paal, and she had only the arrangements to attend to; Ida had weaknesses but she wasn't fickle. Why spend the night here? To pack, of course — she couldn't do it in an hour — and to give more thought to her plans. It *was* a major step. Bee was too like their dad, quick with a reckless opinion.

They had their own life, Bee and Lester, she had intruded enough already; and when would she be able to visit with Mama again?

She wondered if Paal had returned to his beloved shack.

"Come on, Peter, let's go sit by the schoolhouse!"

There was still a bench at the west end of the building. The sun had dried it. Ida would be comfortable here and not seen from the road. She didn't expect many cars to pass, but if even one did the driver would probably recognize her and stop. Chatting might be awkward. And the schoolyard was a good safe place for the child.

She told him to keep off the plowing. His little boots were muddy as it was.

Peter began chasing around the school, each time yelling "Catch me!" But Mama wouldn't join in the game. She only smiled. His circles grew larger and larger until he was struggling through heavy bent weeds. He almost tripped over something, a feathery thing with blood on it, that lay hidden in the tangle. It was brown and gold and red and had a white neck-ring. He saw that the red part wasn't blood; however, there was some dark stuff on the feathers.

"I found a bird, Mama!" He pointed as he looked at her.

Ida came to see. "Know what that is?" she said. "That's a pheasant."

"Is it dead?"

"Ya they must have shot and left it, poor creature."

Ida took a stick and exposed the pheasant's head, a brilliant green; it was intact. But the tail feathers were missing. It had been shot from the rear. Peter said he'd carry it home.

"Ish! Mustn't touch! You never, never play with dead things. The hunters were sposed to carry it home but they didn't, and it's too late. Just let it be. I wish people didn't hunt at all."

"A daddy pheasant or a mama pheasant?"

She stared awhile at the ruined beauty of the bird. "Oh, a daddy pheasant, I guess."

Peter's new game was an exploration of the yard. He wanted to find the mama pheasant too. Mama herself didn't seem interested. She sat with her eyes turned down and her hands together, not watching him.

"Dear God," she was praying, "help me to do as You would have me do, or forgive me the sin I am about to commit. I know it's wrong. It's the child I'm thinking about — and Paal as well. Being married to me hasn't helped him one bit. We're not alike. And if we're unhappy what'll happen to Peter? O Lord, I only want what's best! I beg You lend me Your strength!"

He got close to the edge of the grass, where the tempting field began, and *then* Mama woke up. He heard her warning with pleasure and obeyed, but he didn't retreat. It was fun to be noticed, and he hoped to prolong the sensation by not moving. As she approached, he was worried enough to run and meet her. But he could tell she wasn't mad. Mama had been crying.

"Well, let's go see Gramma," she said.

Ida was tired of moping. She'd use the remainder of the walk to think it out, *hard,* and that was a promise.

As they headed north, she was just as glad that she couldn't see the yard of the estate; too many trees in between. It was so quiet around here, and so unlike Seattle, that a man's voice could be heard a mile away — as long as the wind didn't rise. But there were no human sounds in the air this afternoon.

They could always return to Seattle, she knew the town, Peter was used to it, should things not work out in Fargo. They might be wiser to do so immediately. A person had to be a little daring now and then, or how would she *ever* get anyplace? Ida hoped she had it in her.

The rumble of an engine was growing. She called Peter, held his arm and looked back. It was Uncle Alvin's green Model-A.

Slowly it came to a halt in the middle of the road, then his full nose and tiny smile appeared in the window. "Ya-sah," he said, clicking his tongue.

Since the death of Uncle Carl, Alvin was the only one left at her grandfolks'. Oh Carl's widow hadn't really moved out, and people were talking, but the relatives understood he was sleeping in the shop as usual. Mama had stressed this. Alvin the bachelor underling hadn't ever been off the farm. In middle age he inherited a share of it, and, at Carl's passing, all of the work. His brothers and sisters were gone, so he farmed their shares too and paid them at harvest. To Mama, his position in the family was more important than what might happen to the widow.

Alvin winked at his grand-nephew. The toy tractor which he had brought the other day had been forgotten by neither of them.

"Were you gonna stop at Jensine?" said Ida.

"Na-sah. Have to drive in Mora for to buy medicine, *du vet,* and tomorrow is Sabbath. I might have a nickel for the kid though."

Peter took the warm coin and studied it.

"He sure loves the nice truck you gave him," said Ida. "Say 'thank you Uncle Alvin'."

"It's a tractor," said the little boy.

"Ya-sah!"

Both adults watched Peter and grinned for a moment. Alvin stepped on the gas. The idling engine belched. "Well how goes it with you then?" he said to Ida.

She had been dreading this, sighed before she answered: "Oh it goes — *has* to go. Looking for jobs and houses and trying to get settled and so forth."

She didn't continue. Her Uncle nodded, as though satisfied with that. Again they focused on Peter.

"Spose I can give you a ride," said Alvin, "if you want to hop in, I spose."

"No that's fine, we're just out for a walk, it's not too far, thanks anyway."

The car lurched forward, Alvin smiling and clicking; but he did seem a bit offended. She told Peter to say goodbye.

"Thank you!" he called to the shrinking machine.

Mama's droll brothers had been on "medicine" for years. Everybody had known what Carl and Alvin went to Mora to get, but no one had dared utter the word. The two had been like a couple of schoolkids, giggling, hiding the bottle, whispering even between themselves of "medicine," yet if Ida or Oliver had laughed there would have been awful retribution. They could be mean, all right. Mama hadn't spoken of their drinking; once, however, she had pointed out that the farm work *got done*. True, they weren't regular alcoholics. Now poor Carl was dead, but poor Uncle Alvin hadn't changed one iota. She almost laughed.

Then it struck her that if he met them on the road next week he'd probably drive on by; people didn't talk to a fallen woman. Her amusement vanished with her forgetfulness. She was divorcing Paal. But did she realize what all it *meant?* Had she anticipated the consequences? Hurting and estranging those nearest to her would be one, just one, and she hated to imagine the others. In the silence of this country, where things lay open to God's eye, the thought of divorce seemed unreal. She asked herself what many would soon be asking: How could she?

Ida wanted to keep a home in the world, to merit the tongue-clicks of Uncle Alvin, and the only world happened to be Hedmark, North Dakota. In Seattle a person could get *ten* divorces and it wouldn't matter.

So? She hadn't been forced to leave.

As they cleared the last bunch of trees that hid the yard, Ida's heart was racing. But Papa's Model-A sat alone there.

Papa himself was out on the front steps. He had a magazine in his hand, no coat on; he must have been looking for them.

O.H. Iverson said nothing until they had come within easy range of his voice. When he spoke it was with the indifferent tone of a public official:

"Paal Malmlund called. There's been an accident."

VIII. Minuet In G

This was one hell of an argument. He told her to shut her yap and turn off the damn radio. His head was aching too much to go on. The loud piano music made it worse. Finally his mother said:
When I played this, Stalin signed the Potsdam agreement.
The music had stopped. But that wasn't his mother talking, it was Harry Truman.
They had warned him, the folks, not to drink while tending bar, he'd lose track of the money, but that's what must have happened. Ya that was it, and he had passed out on the floor and another day had come and the President was tickling the ivories. No wonder she got mad, finding him like this. The radio was like a weapon; it'd bring him around and support her argument as well.
The voices continued, but not hers, not Truman's. Where in hell had she gone to now? The floor wasn't soft. Everything hurt: head, back, arms, hands. He sure must have tied one on last night. But if he didn't try to get up and start sweeping, there'd be no peace in this establishment.
His eyes were beginning to work. The folks' place had changed since the fire. It was a strange gray-painted room of three walls. Somehow they had lifted him onto this cot; brothers must have helped, decent of them. He saw blood on his hands and blood on his right forearm, and he knew what the crap on his cheek was.
They had removed the fourth wall and put in iron bars instead.
He was groaning like a sonofabitch. However, he did manage to stand. Once in that position, he discovered he could walk too. The hundred kinds of misery he was in — and he had the aches and the shakes, by golly — didn't include the dry heaves. Thank the Big Man above for that!
They had forgotten to lock the door of the cell. "Some clink," he said as he wandered out into the hall. They don't even turn the key.
He went towards the voices. A heavyset cop, the desk sergeant, was chewing a pencil and listening to the radio.
"Paw Momlin? How you doin?"
It seemed to take a week to answer: "Pretty good, still a little tired."

"Well we got him down the corridor. You gonna press charges?"

Paal's mind wouldn't operate, but he said no quickly, pretending he remembered.

"You sure? The guy *did* attack you. There's witnesses."

"Naw, no need to bother. What time is it?"

The sergeant's pencil indicated a clock on the wall: 11:55, noon already. That didn't mean much either.

"I spose I look plenty rough," said Paal.

"We didn't take you to the hospital, you weren't hurt that bad, and since you're an out-of-towner we couldn't take you home. So we brought you in for the night. You're free to leave." The sergeant aimed his pencil another way. "If you wanna wash up, the room's in there."

Paal entered the john like a man of plaster; to rush would be to crack. "You're made of it too," he said to the white unshaven reflection blinking at him. Those cuts weren't so bad, mere scratches; it was the swellings and blue marks the soap couldn't touch. He'd have to get that hair in place, but no comb. The comb was in the jacket, and no jacket.

His billfold and jacket waited for him on the desk. As he claimed them he ventured a sore smile.

The sergeant did not return it. "You headin' out west?"

"No we just moved back here, you see."

"Better get that driver-license changed, fella, and take it easy on the booze. This happens again, we gotta throw you in the tank."

"Oh ya. Is the Pontiac outside?"

"I didn't even *see* no car."

He traveled some distance from the police station before anything, didn't want a run-in with the guy they'd be releasing, then stepped in an alley to check what he had: the car keys and a buck and a half. It might have been worse. He ran the comb through his matted hair. The sun was out and the snow was melting. Yesterday, the whole damn nightmare, spun in front of him; but he'd rather not think about Ida or the still obscure events of the evening. He should have a slug of coffee first.

The Broadway cafes were all packed for the noon meal, so he tried the lunch counter at the Great Northern depot where the price of a cup brought endless refills and, unless a train arrived, there was little commotion. He'd just sit down and think and figure what to do next.

But the second swallow got him worrying. It was the car — the Pontiac might have been towed. He ought to shoot right over to the Amidon and see. Then there was Ida; remembering her shamed him. It was as though all yesterday had been a part of the drinking — the quarrel, the broken fanbelt, the storm — and he out of character, not fully responsible. That's how it seemed and that's why he felt so low.

That was the kind of trick beer played on memory. He'd better start using his noggin. Fact was, he had not said a *word* to her while under the influence, gone in that there bar alone. When he called they couldn't find a Brandbu listed. Nothing had been said, and just as well. A rowdy bunch those men were; he should have grabbed his nickel and beat it. If that sonofabitching Lyle Iverson —

"More coffee?" said the waitress as she refilled his cup. "You been in a wreck or something?"

Paal nodded and looked at her, but he wasn't really seeing her kind middle-aged face; he was seeing the faces in a picture of his night at the Amidon.

He must've got mad — at the operator? — because when he left the phone he started shouting. About what he couldn't say. There was a man with glasses, young fellow who claimed to be an expert on Marx. Then he denied it and accused Paal of being the one! None of that was too clear. He made it back to where he had been sitting, so much he remembered.

Oh, no, that wasn't it. He spotted Lyle at the far end of the bar and shouted at *him*, told him to leave or else. But Lyle just acted like a stranger. Paal got off the stool and walked over to the sonofabitch — he didn't threaten him — and whispered in his ear, he said, "Bet you screwed a lot of boys in the army." When Lyle turned that pink mug around he saw it *wasn't* Lyle, this guy was different, oh no, but the drinkers had stood aside and whoever he was came on swinging and must've hit lucky because the picture faded about there.

So that's how it was. Uff-da!

"Storm sure quit in a hurry, didn't it?" said the waitress.

Paal's eyes, as he uncovered them, were those of a man who had been sleeping. His voice was that of someone newly born to the world. But there was more surprise than joy in it. "Ya, hit and run I guess."

When he left the counter, the waitress had nothing to do but observe him. He moved with care through the vacant lobby, pausing, as though to rest, at the news stand.

Two killed, three injured in wreck. In a headon collision during the first winter storm of the —

The coffee had been a nickel and so was the paper. He didn't plan to read it, not for awhile at least, but thought he should have something to carry and hang on to.

The platform was like a stretch of desert. Unwinking, the sun looked down from a brute blue sky. He got to where the tracks crossed Broadway and headed south. The Amidon was near Front and Eighth, so he'd follow Broadway to Front and then go west. It's around a mile, he figured, but don't rush; if the car's towed it's towed.

Everyone who had fled the storm was back in public today. Downtown was teeming. Paal had some trouble holding his own in the rush. But he was glad to be surrounded. That man from the bar might be out hunting for him.

While he didn't expect to see Ida, he kept alert anyway.

Some time they'd had, he and Ida. Now that he'd gotten the bar scene straight, he could rehearse the earlier ordeal. It too took the form of pictures: her brown coat wandering towards him in the park; the statue;

a beer bottle flying, then his thermos jug; a speck who vanished in the north; Bee with a paper sack and snow in her face. Paal felt sick all over again.

But he hadn't *said* much amiss, had he? Wasn't it he who'd started to apologize by the silo there? Ya he had been nice as you please, damn it, tailed the woman to her sister's, phoned when he got to the bar; and that was two, no *three* tries he had made. Maybe if she had accepted that phone call, damn it, the rest wouldn't have happened.

Remembering there was no Brandbu listed, he socked his leg. God he was cranky! He stuck a thumb in his shirt pocket and didn't find a thing; it wasn't in his jacket or pants either.

He went into the Powers Hotel and bought a can of snoose. It was thirteen cents, a penny more than it should have been. The remaining buck twenty-seven would be enough though; with the car towed and no gas to buy, it'd be a lot. He didn't want to worry until he knew. A big comforting pinch would hold him for the moment.

The street's glare didn't bother him now and he was up to the business of walking in it. He was even prepared to meet Ida. Say hello is what he'd do, act as though nothing's wrong. How are you today? and so forth. His appearance would get the rest across to her.

Paul smoothed his hair, took in his belt a notch and yawned. These trousers were loose as hell. He hadn't had a bite to eat since God knows when — at the bar? — and here he had almost forgotten the meaning of hunger.

Other splinters of the night poked at his brain. Words had been said there, said and tossed back by a man laughing. Oh ya: *livet er et hus*. He had seen the truth and spoken, but in English, then some gutless character switched to *norsk*. Whether it was *livet er et hus* or life is a house, the remark had seemed pretty important at the time, even if it made less sense now than the argument he had dreamed in jail.

He retreated from the edge of the curb and walked along the store fronts instead. Someone who'd gotten off as easy as he shouldn't take unnecessary chances. In this town, a drunken blabbermouth wasn't too popular. He'd simply have to go his way and keep inconspicuous until he was out of it.

At 1:25 he was in the middle of a bunch of people at the corner of Eighth and Front. He saw the Pontiac, calm and shiny and his; but it sat awfully near to the Amidon. As the light turned green and they began to cross, Paal darted over and got in and thrust his key in the switch. The engine started. He drove away, putting that damn bar behind him for good.

He continued down Eighth to the rich man's district, then parked to do a little thinking. Only respectable folks lived here, not the sort who'd know and bother *him*. He rested his hot forehead on the hot steering wheel and breathed. "Well we made it," he told the car.

This had been the big thing, saving the Pontiac; this done, he could attend to the somehow lesser worry of Ida.

The gas-gauge needle was a hair over E. He had a dollar twenty-seven cents. Stick fuel in the tank and fuel in the stomach and that'll be it, he thought. Once they settled all this, he could have a plain ordinary good night's sleep.

He might as well catch a nap right here. But soon as he lay down he got to figuring, and when the answer came to him he wasn't so tired anymore.

It was a short but slow trip to a filling station at the edge of town. Paal asked the man for sixty cents' worth of regular and the use of the telephone. Since there was no exchange at Hedmark, the call would go to Mora, Minnesota, just over the Red, and cost him most of what nickels he had left.

But eating was no longer a concern.

"Hellaw!" Iverson talkin!"

"Ya is Ida there then?"

"Hah?"

"It's Paal! I say is Ida around!"

"Who?!"

"This here is Paal and I wanna speak to Ida!"

"Oh."

The old man was discussing it off the line. Paal waited in a sweat. She was home.

"No she's outside vith *brodern,*" said O.H., "and ve don't know vhere."

"Well just tell her I got in a car accident and I'm okay, but I have to come out and I'll be there this afternoon."

"Hah?!"

"I got in a car accident and I'm coming out there!"

"Are you in the hospital then?"

"Tell her I'm coming!"

"Oh. Awright."

He paid and took off in a hurry. Just trying to talk to that old jackass spoiled a person's mood. It was the hollering that did it.

As he entered the country he felt good though. The earth was dark where snow had melted, and the air clear; sure different from yesterday. The newspaper lay on the seat staring up at him: *Two killed, three injured.* Ya it could have been worse. A person had to be thankful. He hoped Ida would agree.

After one more necessary stop, at the shanty, he would be on the road. The track around the field was a bit soft now, but he reached the silo without getting stuck. He positioned the car so that it couldn't be seen from the highway.

Paal didn't like what he was about to do; it had to be done, however, so no sense shilly-shallying. He opened the rumble seat and took out the larger of his jacks, the bumper jack, and carried it to the right front fender. "Here goes your looks," he said through clenched teeth as he raised the jack and struck.

Here goes that nice paint job — there went the headlight too, goddam it!

Quitting was harder than beginning, but when he had created enough evidence he stood back and panted. She looked hit, all right. Yessir, she's been in a minor collision, all right. As a perfecting touch, he made a dent in the bumper.

He scanned the field and the river woods and the shack and the distant highway. There had been no witnesses, not even that red mutt.

Paal was so tired he'd have welcomed the grave, but there was one last item: the thermos. He found it near the silo. It was chipped and it rattled. He'd bring the thermos jug along as further inspiring evidence.

IX. Soap and Iodine

Peter liked driving his tractor on the sill. It was bright and warm, a street with soldiers marching to the King's house. A street meant cars could go there too, up and down as they did in Seattle. But the King lived far, far over the ocean. Mama said Norway. *Those soldiers have been in the war.* Seattle was in the war, and *he* lived there. Now everybody was marching home, Johnny and the Pontiac and the soldiers — the King must be their grandpa — and they wouldn't see the ocean anymore.

Outside were trees. *My such beautiful scenes from Norway.* Mama didn't tell him the tree picture's name. Probably it didn't need one. The sun came out of the branches through the window, lighting the sill and a big patch on the floor of what Mama and Gramma called the south room. The patch was a field in North Dakota.

In the shadow along the sill's inside edge he imagined trees and houses. That's how it would look by a street in Seattle or Oslo, *as in days of yore.* But the sill was too narrow for the tractor; he had to drive with half a back tire off it. There were no tractors in Seattle. Maybe they weren't supposed to go there. Uncle Alvin drove a tractor and gave him this one, and Uncle Alvin was in North Dakota.

Peter hated to leave but thought he'd better. What if he had an accident? "There's been an accident," Grandpa would say, and Mama would scream and run in the house. He didn't want that. Gripping his toy, he left the busy sill, went down through valleys and mountains and crossed the dark ocean of the floor to North Dakota. He wouldn't hit any cars in the field. But he'd have to watch out for birds.

Uncle Avin's nickel remained in his left hand. It was hot and shiny. He set it on the patch. As they came from seeing the dead pheasant and Uncle Alvin, Mama told him, "Let me have the nickel now and I'll stick it in your piggy bank so you don't lose it." That's what she did with the money people gave him. Sometimes she turned it into sweets. But when Grandpa said "There's been an accident," she must have forgotten, and here the nickel lay. He steered around and around it. Maybe it still was Uncle Alvin's.

Peter could hear them talking, Mama and Gramma in the kitchen and Grandpa in the kitchen door. Mama stopped crying a long time ago.

"Well I spose if he could call he's not in too bad shape. He might have wrecked the car though, and that'll really set us back. We just can't afford that right now."

"Ya you know about Mildred's husband after she left — drinking and trouble with the sheriff and losing his job. The poor man was just beside himself. When they start running around, things *always* go wrong."

"He didn't give us enough particulars, so the best ve can do is vait until the facts are *in."*

"Uff-da I wish he'd hurry up and come! I can't stand this."

"You can well be thankful he's alive; and the car must be working, don't you think?"

Peter saw an accident in Seattle. One car bumped another car onto the sidewalk. They didn't move. Men and women and the police stood arguing. An ambulance took somebody away. He heard the siren. Now, as he plowed his field, he was listening for it again.

The only sound that came was a faint, familiar clanging. In Seattle, that meant Daddy's home. The Pontiac was not like most cars. It said *rattle* and *clang*. Peter stopped the tractor and went to the east window. "Daddy's in the yard!"

"Oh he's here?"

"Paal Malmlund's here! Ve better take a look vhat happened."

He thought he should go out and be the first to meet Daddy, but Grandpa was in the door, Mama and Gramma next, so he had to follow. Daddy was leaning against the Pontiac on the driver's side and smiling at the porch. He had cuts and hurts and whiskers. If Peter got in an accident, *he'd* try to smile too.

"There's the little man!" said Daddy. But Peter ran straight to the smashed headlight and began examining. Mama told him not to touch it.

They viewed the damage in silence, O.H. with his hands in his pockets, Ida and Jensine with arms folded. It was a mild but an autumn afternoon, the sun retreating, yet the dampness of the air seemed not to bother them. All eyes were for the Pontiac, which sat there in greater discomfort. They didn't watch Paal as he came around to offer testimony.

"She still rolls, at least," he said, gently kicking the right front tire. Ida and Jensine shook their heads.

"Vell have you been charged then?" said O.H. Iverson.

Paal's smile was steady. "Nooo, it wasn't like that; no trouble involved. I had supper in Fargo last night and was planning to stay over with a man who lives south of town. I was just driving there, you know."

"Vell you must have hit something, that's all I can say."

"Was it only the fender, I hope?" said Ida.

"Ya I was turning in at his road and I hit this ice, you see, and went in the ditch. That wouldn't have been so bad, but he had an old plow there and it got in the way."

"Oooohhh," said Jensine.

The man who owned the shack had indeed a rusted plow in his ditch; Paal had taken note of it. He smoothed his hair with shaky fingers and continued: "There wasn't much I could do — it was late — so I walked to that fellow's house and cleaned up and spent the night, then he helped me get her going this morning. It's not serious, you know; the engine's fine."

Peter was next to Ida. "What happened to the tractor?" No one seemed to hear him.

"Thank heaven it wasn't any worse," said Ida.

That was true; Paal had to hide his relief. But now he could show his exhaustion. If they bought *one* wreck, they'd buy another. As he stretched he looked at his arms. "I came out pretty good too, just a few bumps and twisted muscles."

Their eyes were for him at last, and the women's sympathies. But O.H. didn't like what he saw. "I spose you vere drinking —"

"You got to put medicine on him, Ida, and that's all there is to it. He might get infected." Jensine's harsh tone overrode the critic, who suddenly chose to retire. O.H. went muttering toward the house.

"No I'm fine," said Paal, modest in victory. However, he didn't object when they led him to the back door. The spoils awaited him inside: food and rest.

Peter was held by the wonder of the wreck. Cars didn't go in the field and tractors didn't go in the street. Uncle Alvin tied a plow to his tractor, so plows went in the field. Nothing went in a ditch. It was too steep. Daddy and the plow were not supposed to be in the ditch. It got in the way, Daddy said. What happened to the tractor?

He expected Mama and Gramma to call his name; he didn't have a jacket. But they were taking Daddy to put medicine on him and forgot. He could go as close to the wreck as he wanted. The fender had a whole bunch of little dents in it, and some dents were green. He remembered that the Pontiac used to be green, then Daddy painted it black. Paint wasn't sharp. He could touch it as much as he wanted. But the dents didn't feel very good.

He put his knees on the bumper and his hands on the grille. The Pontiac breathed out warm, like Mama. Every car had a face. The grille was its mouth and the headlights were its eyes. Some cars smiled and others frowned; he still wasn't sure about the Pontiac.

One of its eyes was broken. The silver ring didn't have much glass in it. Glass was sharp; he mustn't touch. *Don't rub your eyes.* But the ring was smooth.

The porch door creaked open and there was Grandpa in his black coat. Peter went up to him but didn't cry. That would be wrong.

"There's been a accident," he said with a smile.

O.H. Iverson inspected the pearl of blood that was forming on the tiny fingertip. "An accident, hah? Vell you just go in the kitchen vith everybody else. They got a regular hospital in there."

He couldn't stand any more womenfolks' clucking and cooing or the whimpering of Paal, so he had fled to where it was quiet. O.H. moved in circles through the darkening day, uncertain of his path. He'd rather not be out at all, he had walked enough; he wanted to finish that magazine; but they wouldn't let him. Chasing around and drinking and wrecking cars they knew how to do. They had yet to learn to behave themselves in company. Their troubles were of *no* interest to him. It was Jensine who enjoyed meddling in people's affairs. Well he'd throw them out, both Ida and her so-called husband, and read in peace. He'd give that old hen something to squawk about!

Men were meant to rest at this hour, gather to the hearth; so it had been since ancient times. But he was slogging through the mud as if he belonged in it — O.H. Iverson, attorney. Ahead of him lay a chunk of gumbo that must have been dragged in on Paal's car. It dispersed when he kicked it. *"Ut* and to hell with you!" he said.

He halted by the wooden tub. The tub was almost empty. He waited until he remembered. Oh ya: he had brought peanuts from town and stuck them in a can in the shed. Tomorrow, he was planning to —

"Can't even feed the sqvirrels vhen you vant!" he said, cursing, as he went to get the peanuts.

Paal, having removed his dirty shirt, sat backwards on a chair while Ida cleaned his wounds and treated them with iodine. Jensine was cooking supper but observed whenever she had a minute. The air smelled of coffee and boiling potatoes.

The medication done, Ida began to check the swellings. She had the voice and manner of a nurse. "This one here hurt?"

"Yaaa, I can feel it."

"Didn't break the skin like on your cheek though."

Jensine was the doctor: *"Nei* we should have had ice for that."

"I should be all right, it'll go down."

"Must have been a *terrific* impact," said Ida.

"I hit the wheel, you know — and the dash."

"Lucky you didn't go through the windshield."

"Ya you can say that again."

Ida wasn't thinking of how it had been when Papa told her the news, the horror and the guilt she had experienced; her immediate task absorbed everything. That was the nature of work. Poor Paal, such scrapes he got into! But she wasn't unaware of her growing contentment.

Peter's dramatic arrival, his happy presentation of a bleeding finger, called for a rebuke. Mama was the shocked one:

"What oh what did you do?"

"A accident," said the grinning child.

Ida spoke to him as darkly as she could. "Were you playing around the car after all?"

"Soap and iodine, quick!" said Mama. "He might have lockjaw!"

Gramma was already tending to him, so Peter didn't have to answer for himself. He submitted to the sting of the liquid without complaint, but he was avoiding Mama's eye.

"So the kid was in an accident too," said Daddy.

Peter sensed that they weren't angry at him. If he kept on smiling, they would smile.

"There. Now leave the bandage alone." Gramma wasn't smiling.

But, when he finally dared to peek at Mama, he saw that she and Daddy were. Daddy rubbed his face.

"We'll have a bite to eat, then you can sleep," said Mama.

"I spose I can shave in the morning then."

The lord of the eastern estate, having finished at the tub, was about to re-enter. He'd do so by way of the porch; walking through the kitchen might give them the wrong idea. They were unwanted here and he'd have them know it.

The odors in the house disturbed him. Those who ate and drank what had been boiled half to death were idiots, and because of the idiots he'd have to wait for his tea. O.H. tossed his coat on the sofa, lighted his pipe and sank into the rocker. At least they weren't gabbing.

The rocker stopped. O.H. appeared in the kitchen door.

Jensine and Ida and Peter and Paal were feeding quietly by lamplight. The only one to raise his head was Peter.

"Awright, Paal," said O.H., "how much money you gonna borrow from us?"

Ida answered: "Oh let him be. He's had plenty to contend with as it is."

He stared at her in confusion. Never had she addressed him so. This was Jensine's daughter, he could see that. "I vasn't talking to you!"

"Well I'm talking to you, Papa," said Ida, her chin out. "This has gone far enough."

Dreading trouble from elsewhere, O.H. began to withdraw. He didn't fear Jensine's tongue; it was just that he had heard her too often. The familiarity of the words made him sick. Still, she caught him:

"You'd think they would be civil to members of the family, if no one else. They can do their bragging and criticizing in town."

"Yayayayayayaya!" he said to himself in the next room.

Paal had been looking at his food all the while, but Peter seemed upset. Ida stroked him. "Just don't worry about anything, we're gonna finish our supper and that's that."

Mean old sonofabitch, Paal thought. Some other time I would have gone for him, like he was hoping. Lucky I'm dead on my ass. Could've missed a night's sleep there.

Ida amazed herself, standing up to Papa as she did. Her rage in that instant annulled her timidity, and she was *right*. It was as though she hadn't been right before. The passing of the anger should have brought regret, but her mood didn't change. She glanced at Mama's mouth: a straight line there would indicate the real situation. The smile she saw was a blessing. Her husband and her son were a blessing. It was nice to come home, but it was nice *not* to be a daughter anymore.

As they were doing the dishes, the phone emitted one long and three short. She didn't even think of letting Papa answer.

"Hello again," said Bee.

"Hello. Are you back in Fargo?"

The rubbernecks' interference made it hard to hear and harder to talk.

"Ya we're home. I was just going to say, I'm sorry we rushed off like that."

Ida understood. Bee meant that she was sorry about losing her temper. "Oh that was fine, that was nothing."

"You can tell Mama for me."

"Fine, I'll do that. He showed up, you know. He was in a. . .he had a problem with the car."

"Oh?"

"He's all right, though, and the car too. Everything seems to be all right. I guess we'll. . .we'll be coming in pretty soon."

"My," said Bee, full of knowledge, "that didn't take long."

"We'll try and stop by so we can visit." The static was maddening. The groans of the rocking chair didn't help. Ida plugged an ear. "You sound a thousand miles away. I *wish* they had a better phone system in Mora."

"It isn't the system!" Bee shouted. "It's that snoopy Mrs. Peterson and all the rest!"

There was noise on the line. Ida and Bee ended giggling, as they had so often in their old innocent days.

Peter chewed a molasses cookie and watched Mama. The laughing colored her cheeks red. She told Gramma a story — *Bee, snoopy Mrs. Peterson* — and Gramma nodded but she didn't laugh. She only clicked her tongue.

After the phone rang, Daddy went outside. Now he stood at the foot of the stairs and he was smiling. "I guess I'll quit early," he said.

Mama was drying cups with a towel. Her cheeks looked better. "Ya you need to. I'll be up in awhile."

He had a white bandage on his finger. Blood was red. Mama's white cheeks turned red when she laughed. That wasn't good.

His tractor was in the south room but he was afraid to leave. He thought he should stay in the kitchen. Mama and Gramma put the dishes on the shelves and talked. Once Mama laughed. But she didn't act funny.

"I wish Bee hadn't," said Gramma. "Doesn't she know Mrs. Peterson's head of ladies' aid?"

"It serves the old bag right, that's my opinion."

Then Mama took off her apron and said what he feared: "I think he should sleep down here tonight. We can put bedding on the couch."

"Or he can be with me, just as well."

Mama and Daddy and Peter slept in the same room, they in a big bed and he on a cot. If Daddy was gone he slept with Mama. That's how it was supposed to be.

"You say your prayers for Gramma tonight," she said, hugging him, "and we'll see you in the morning."

But he followed Mama to the stairs. "I want to sleep on my own cot. I'm not snoopy."

Ida had thought she was laughed out; she'd been wrong. The first seizure seemed mild compared to this one. That little tyke — was there anything he didn't notice? The unknowing faces of her audience of two were an added provocation. She had to look at the wall to get herself under control.

"Of *course* you're not," she said, meeting his indignant gaze. "But Daddy and I want to be alone and talk. That's what big people like to do; that's what you'll do when *you're* big. Now you stay with Gramma just this once, and tomorrow I'll buy you a treat. Won't that be good? Nighty-night, Peter."

The owlet didn't reply as his grandmother took him captive. Oh we'll make it up to him, thought Ida, afire with various loves.

Each step had its own squeak; so did each board upstairs. Her hand reached the door of the bedroom. Paal had left it ajar; this meant that she was to close it. Entering, she did so.

While she was undressing in the lightless warm air, he coughed and moaned. She figured he'd still be awake. But nothing was said until she crept in next to him.

Paal began: "Wish I could find a soft spot here."

"You're pretty sore, I imagine."

"Ya, and stiff too."

He hadn't intended to joke, and gave a second moan for clarification.

Whispering was easier than talking; whispering also eased their silences.

"We've been through quite a couple days, haven't we?" she said.

"I guess we have."

"I'm so worn out and exhausted I hardly know what to do."

"It wasn't any fun, that's for sure."

"At least the weather's improved."

"Ya that's one thing."

"Well I've been thinking about that place you rented."

"I should have seen it wasn't fit to live in. I'll have to try and get out of the deal."

"Well it's not my dream house, but I've been thinking we could always fix it up — as long as the weather's improved and so on."

The rhythm of Paal's breathing slowed. He hadn't counted on *this* major a victory. It'd be wise to mind his tongue. "We could always do that, I spose," he said.

"I'll borrow some mops and rags and buckets and stuff from Mama and we can go and start in in the morning."

"Ya it's gonna be a pleasant day, I understand."

Ida knew it wouldn't be such a pleasant day at the eastern estate, but now that she had decided she was at the mercy of no one.

Their whispering had ceased. Paal's arm brushed hers as though by accident.

O.H. Iverson didn't speak, just marched through the kitchen and out. He'd empty his bladder at the usual site, west of the shed. From there he could survey the sky.

Cool and clear it was, and the starshine brilliant. Tomorrow would be fair.

Reading in Gjerset's history had distracted him from the concerns of the household; he'd gone preoccupied through the kitchen, not angry. As he buttoned up, however, it all returned.

Quite a daughter Jensine had raised! In ancient times they had a remedy for women's insolence. A father was *not* to be contradicted, that was that; and *he* had never thrown her doll in the stove!

Jensine had only the coffee cup to aim her eyes at, but she was able to ignore his entrance anyway. Peter was moving his yellow tractor on the table.

"Vell, *brodern*," said O.H. as he mounted the steps, "vhat do you think of the vorld you came into?" His tone was both doting and sarcastic.

Her mother had been the last to bed and the first up, and Jensine continued the tradition. She enjoyed those two periods of solitude. In the early hours she could plan the day without interruption, and after everyone was asleep she could review the accomplishments of it. Oh, she didn't resent her loved ones; she served them, preparing food and fire, even as they slumbered. It wasn't easy to concentrate when they were about, that's all. But Jensine did resent O.H. and was never sorry to see him vanish. With him out of the road, the coffee tasted sweeter.

The little tractor wasn't going very fast.

"It's Peter's bedtime," she said, lifting him before he had a chance to object. "You'll sleep in Gramma's room, and oh for cozy!"

She got him in with no fussing. Must be too tired to talk, she figured — not that O.H. had deserved a reply. But he did say *now I lay me down to sleep,* the prayer which Ida, who had learned it from Jensine herself, taught him. She tucked the quilt around his body and gave him a kiss.

"Night, Gramma," he said. "Wake me if they go."

Most of what she'd had to do, in the kitchen and elsewhere, had been done. She ought to have washed Paal's shirt so he could have it in the morning. It should be soaked, though; the stains were terrible. Taking rain water from a jug, she filled the dishpan and kneaded the shirt into it. She'd do the scrubbing tomorrow, then hang it on the line. He had plenty other things to wear.

Now she was free to dwell on the greatest accomplishment. Jensine knew that Ida and Paal would be leaving together; that was certain. The day had not been wasted. Now she could savor a cup of coffee along with the thought.

But first she'd bow her head and thank God Almighty for curing Ida of her silliness.

Peter dreamed that he and Mama and Daddy were in the car rolling down a hill, and it was evening, and at the bottom was the edge of the sea, and the water looked huge and flat and purple. *We're gonna drive into the ocean,* said Daddy. Peter hung onto Mama and shrieked.

X. Home River

The cold has inspired lingering ducks to go on south but hasn't frozen the moving surface of the water. It will take more than a snap to do that. Even the ice that edged the banks has dissolved into the current which now at October's end is inching along as it did in August, and a little higher. The woods are open. Many birds have left but those that remain can be seen: jay, crow, nuthatch, chickadee, log cock, junco. Deer-time is coming, a season of gray slanting light and splashes of blood on the gray earth. But for the moment the light is copper, and there's nothing to hurry the animals.

A big skinny red dog is guzzling water, his forepaws in the mud. The deer may be at peace; he's not. His nervousness and hanging tail show that he doesn't belong here.

The man he trusted brought him to the outskirts of Fargo and tied him to a post and drove away. He cut the rope with his teeth; however, he did not abandon the neighborhood. After every hunting trip to the woods or the garbage cans, he returned to check the post.

Last night he dined on rabbit and slept well. His hunger was back this morning. The man still hadn't come, so he ran to the woods for more game. All he has gotten is thirsty.

The dog's ears arch up. He scrambles to higher ground to wait, staring at the top of the incline. No one lives in the small house there; he's never found garbage around it. Wind stirs the dead vegetation. But it wasn't that he heard, it was a clanging. As he hears another he thinks of the man who threw him bread. Soon he recognizes the voice but stays alert. The dog has been shot at.

Paal carries a scythe on his shoulder and bucket in his hand. With the first he'll cut the standing weeds around the shack; the second is for bearing water to Ida. He has put some tools and a can of nails and a hammer inside the bucket. When the scything's done, he'll fix the outhouse.

He strides with a smile into the good morning sun, keeping ahead of Ida and the boy; the blade he's got is dangerous; no sense taking risks at such a time.

Rising early, he patted Ida on the knee and said he was going to shave. Before he did, however, he went out to the Pontiac to fetch that thermos jug and toss it. If she saw it she might think he was trying to remind her of something — the very thing the two of them had just managed so well to forget. Then he noticed his shirt drying on the line and knew that the battle was over. Let O.H. Iverson say whatever he liked: Paal had Jensine behind him.

Ida decided to bring Peter along and that was fine. The trip was fine, too; it seemed they all were supposed to be together for a change, heading where they were supposed to go. Ida sang "When Johnny Comes Marching Home" and Paal joined in, though it was a different tune he'd rather have been singing.

He parked beyond the silo, towards the shack. There might still be breadcrumbs in the dirt, and avoiding the place'd hurt no one.

Paal doesn't have much to worry about except the landlord, who figures in his tale of the accident. They saw the ditched plow. The kid wanted to stop for a closer look but he put him off, saying they had work to do. Paal will talk to the landlord before Ida gets a chance, tell him he made up the story to appease the wife, and ask him, as a man of the world, to go along with it. That shouldn't be too hard.

On this kind of morning it's hard to worry. There's a soft southwest wind, not a fleck in the sky, and an honest job waiting. At the bottom of the hill is the stubborn old river, and it's quite a sight — and seems they'll be having a guest as well.

"See the doggy, Peter?" he says. "He's coming to visit. Hello, red guy!"

The dog is awful big and strange. Holding tight the lunch sack Mama gave him to carry, Peter walks right next to her. Now the dog is sitting. He hopes it won't move.

He had been watching Daddy shave and Mama came downstairs and said they were all going to *the new house*. Gramma didn't argue. She just told Mama to put extra clothes on him and be sure he didn't get into any more sharp things. Then they loaded the poor car with Gramma's stuff and drove rattling onto the road.

Mama was singing too much to answer his every question, but she did say the *the new house* wasn't in Norway or Seattle. "Nope, we're gonna live in the most beautiful place on earth, our beloved Red River valley!"

They passed the plow. The ditch it sat in wasn't very steep. But the car kept going; Daddy wouldn't listen. "This afternoon, maybe," he said as the plow got littler behind them.

The track is full of gopher diggings, brown and yellow. The shed they're approaching has weeds all around it. This must be the dog's home.

"Where's the new house?" says Peter.

Mama and Daddy laugh.

Ida is lugging a pail, a broom, a mop, a soap-carton and a bundle of rags, but that's not the end of it; the heaviest item is a coal shovel.

She knows what to expect. No broom could get at *those* floors. She'll take out the bottles and the rest of the junk and use the shovel, then sweep.

Yet her heart isn't burdened. It's ringing with march music.

> *Get ready for the Jubilee,*
> *   Hurrah, hurrah!*
> *We'll give the hero three times three,*
> *   Hurrah, hurrah!*

She thinks of Mama's shy smile over breakfast. The table seemed so wide. Their marching had already begun, left, right, left, right, and Mama sensed it too.

Doesn't Paal look like a soldier?

> *The laurel wreath is ready now*
> *To place upon his loyal brow;*
> *And we'll all feel gay*
> *When Johnny comes marching home.*

As she waits for him to unlock the door, her heart is still ringing in tempo.

Ida goes to it. The only way to finish is to start. Hauling and scooping and mopping quicken the tempo, and her song becomes a jig.

They didn't bring a watch, but it must be early afternoon when she steps outside.

Paal has been hammering on the toilet. Peter and the dog are with him there.

"Shall we have something to eat?" she calls.

Peter has made a friend. But he's not sorry to leave the dog and run to Mama. There are cookies in the lunch sack.

The view is wondrous; she's never known the river to be so glassy. It's always moving on yet always where it belongs.

Paal has trimmed the slope and made a regular park of it. This will be their home.

The child comes toward her, a shade uncertain in his eyes.

"Bet you thought Mama had forgotten you," she says. "Let's have a picnic. I haven't quite got rid of the smell in the house yet. Were you touching the dog? I'll wash your hands by the pump."

Paal is grinning, and now she can see the nice dimples in his cheeks. He has his weaknesses, poor guy, but Lord what a handsome man.

Ya well at least I have a cute wife, he tells himself. Even the sweat and the dust and that old bandanna can't hide the fact. His private tune is about ready to be sung:

> *I was so very fond of Nikolina*
> *and Nikolina just as fond of me!*

The red dog circles the pump, where the members of his new life are gathering.